W9-BOA-110

Novel

ALSO BY JULIE OTSUKA

When the Emperor Was Divine

THE BUDDHA IN THE ATTIC

The Buddha in the Attic

Julie Otsuka

Alfred A. Knopf   New York 2011

THIS IS A BORZOI BOOK
PUBLISHED BY ALFRED A. KNOPF

www.aaknopf.com

Knopf, Borzoi Books, and the colophon are registered trademarks of
Random House, Inc.

Chapters of this novel were originally published in slightly different form in
the following magazines: "Come, Japanese!" and "The Children" in Granta
and "Whites" in Harper's.

Library of Congress Cataloging-in-Publication Data

Otsuka, Julie, [date]
The Buddha in the attic / Julie Otsuka.—1st ed.
p.   cm.
"This is a Borzoi book."
ISBN 978-0-307-70000-1
1. Mail-order brides—Fiction. 2. Japanese—California—Fiction.
3. San Francisco (Calif.)—History—20th century—Fiction.
I. Title
PS3615.T88B83 2011
813'.6—dc22   2011013568

Jacket photograph by John Clark
Jacket design by Gabriele Wilson

Manufactured in the United States of America

FIRST EDITION

For Andy

There be of them, that have left a name behind them, that their praises might be reported. And some there be, which have no memorial; who are perished, as though they had never been; and are become as though they had never been born; and their children after them.

—ECCLESIASTICUS 44:8–9

Barn's burnt down—
now
I can see the moon.

—MASAHIDE

THE BUDDHA IN THE ATTIC

COME, JAPANESE!

On the boat we were mostly virgins. We had long black hair and flat wide feet and we were not very tall. Some of us had eaten nothing but rice gruel as young girls and had slightly bowed legs, and some of us were only fourteen years old and were still young girls ourselves. Some of us came from the city, and wore stylish city clothes, but many more of us came from the country and on the boat we wore the same old kimonos we'd been wearing for years—faded hand-me-downs from our sisters that had been patched and redyed many times. Some of us came from the mountains, and had never before seen the sea, except for in pictures, and some of us were the daughters of fishermen who had been around the sea all our lives. Perhaps we had lost a brother or father to the sea, or a fiancé, or perhaps someone we loved had jumped into the water one unhappy morning and simply swum away, and now it was time for us, too, to move on.

ON THE BOAT the first thing we did—before deciding who we liked and didn't like, before telling each other which one of the islands we were from, and why we were leaving, before even bothering to learn each other's names—was compare photographs of our husbands. They were handsome young men with dark eyes and full heads of hair and skin that was smooth and unblemished. Their chins were strong. Their posture, good. Their noses were straight and high. They looked like our brothers and fathers back home, only better dressed, in gray frock coats and fine Western three-piece suits. Some of them were standing on sidewalks in front of wooden A-frame houses with white picket fences and neatly mowed lawns, and some were leaning in driveways against Model T Fords. Some were sitting in studios on stiff high-backed chairs with their hands neatly folded and staring straight into the camera, as though they were ready to take on the world. All of them had promised to be there, waiting for us, in San Francisco, when we sailed into port.

ON THE BOAT, we often wondered: Would we like them? Would we love them? Would we recognize them from their pictures when we first saw them on the dock?

ON THE BOAT we slept down below, in steerage, where it was filthy and dim. Our beds were narrow metal racks stacked one on top of the other and our mattresses were hard and thin and darkened with the stains of other journeys, other lives. Our pillows were stuffed with dried wheat hulls. Scraps of food littered the passageways between berths and the floors were wet and slick. There was one porthole, and in the evening, after the hatch was closed, the darkness filled with whispers. *Will it hurt?* Bodies tossed and turned beneath the blankets. The sea rose and fell. The damp air stifled. At night we dreamed of our husbands. We dreamed of new wooden sandals and end-less bolts of indigo silk and of living, one day, in a house with a chimney. We dreamed we were lovely and tall. We dreamed we were back in the rice paddies, which we had so desperately wanted to escape. The rice paddy dreams were always nightmares. We dreamed of our older and prettier sisters who had been sold to the geisha houses by our fathers so that the rest of us might eat, and when we woke we were gasping for air. *For a second I thought I was her.*

OUR FIRST FEW DAYS on the boat we were seasick, and could not keep down our food, and had to make repeated trips to the railing. Some of us were so dizzy we could not even walk, and lay in our berths in a dull stupor, unable to remember our own names, not to mention those of our new husbands. *Remind me one more time, I'm Mrs. Who?* Some of us clutched our stomachs and prayed out loud to Kannon, the goddess of mercy—*Where are you?*—while others of us preferred to turn silently green. And often, in the middle of the night, we were jolted awake by a violent swell and for a brief moment we had no idea where we were, or why our beds would not stop moving, or why our hearts were pounding with such dread. *Earthquake* was the first thought that usually came to our minds. We reached out for our mothers then, in whose arms we had slept until the morning we left home. Were they sleeping now? Were they dreaming? Were they thinking of us night and day? Were they still walking three steps behind our fathers on the streets with their arms full of packages while our fathers carried nothing at all? Were they secretly envious of us for sailing away? *Didn't I give you everything?* Had they remembered to air out our old kimonos? Had they remembered to feed the cats? Had they made sure to tell us everything we needed to know? *Hold your teacup with both hands, stay out of the sun, never say more than you have to.*

MOST OF US on the boat were accomplished, and were sure we would make good wives. We knew how to cook and sew. We knew how to serve tea and arrange flowers and sit quietly on our flat wide feet for hours, saying absolutely nothing of substance at all. *A girl must blend into a room: she must be present without appearing to exist.* We knew how to behave at funerals, and how to write short, melancholy poems about the passing of autumn that were exactly seventeen syllables long. We knew how to pull weeds and chop kindling and haul water, and one of us—the rice miller's daughter—knew how to walk two miles into town with an eighty-pound sack of rice on her back without once breaking into a sweat. *It's all in the way you breathe.* Most of us had good manners, and were extremely polite, except for when we got mad and cursed like sailors. Most of us spoke like ladies most of the time, with our voices pitched high, and pretended to know much less than we did, and whenever we walked past the deckhands we made sure to take small, mincing steps with our toes turned properly in. Because how many times had our mothers told us: *Walk like the city, not like the farm!*

ON THE BOAT we crowded into each other's bunks every night and stayed up for hours discussing the unknown

continent ahead of us. The people there were said to eat
nothing but meat and their bodies were covered with hair
(we were mostly Buddhist, and did not eat meat, and only
had hair in the appropriate places). The trees were enormous. The plains were vast. The women were loud and
tall—a full head taller, we had heard, than the tallest of our
men. The language was ten times as difficult as our own
and the customs were unfathomably strange. Books were
read from back to front and soap was used in the bath.
Noses were blown on dirty cloths that were stuffed back
into pockets only to be taken out later and used again and
again. The opposite of white was not red, but black. What
would become of us, we wondered, in such an alien land?
We imagined ourselves—an unusually small people armed
only with our guidebooks—entering a country of giants.
Would we be laughed at? Spat on? Or, worse yet, would
we not be taken seriously at all? But even the most reluc-
tant of us had to admit that it was better to marry a
stranger in America than grow old with a farmer from the
village. Because in America the women did not have to
work in the fields and there was plenty of rice and firewood for all. And wherever you went the men held open
the doors and tipped their hats and called out, "Ladies
first" and "After you."

SOME OF US on the boat were from Kyoto, and were delicate and fair, and had lived our entire lives in darkened
rooms at the back of the house. Some of us were from
Nara, and prayed to our ancestors three times a day, and
swore we could still hear the temple bells ringing. Some of

us were farmers' daughters from Yamaguchi with thick wrists and broad shoulders who had never gone to bed after nine. Some of us were from a small mountain hamlet in Yamanashi and had only recently seen our first train. Some of us were from Tokyo, and had seen everything, and spoke beautiful Japanese, and did not mix much with any of the others. Many more of us were from Kagoshima and spoke in a thick southern dialect that those of us from Tokyo pretended we could not understand. Some of us were from Hokkaido, where it was snowy and cold, and would dream of that white landscape for years. Some of us were from Hiroshima, which would later explode, and were lucky to be on the boat at all though of course we did not then know it. The youngest of us was twelve, and from the eastern shore of Lake Biwa, and had not yet begun to bleed. *My parents married me off for the betrothal money.* The oldest of us was thirty-seven, and from Niigata, and had spent her entire life taking care of her invalid father, whose recent death made her both happy and sad. *I knew I could marry only if he died.* One of us was from Kumamoto, where there were no more eligible men—all of the eligible men had left the year before to find work in Manchuria—and felt fortunate to have found any kind of husband at all. *I took one look at his photograph and told the matchmaker, "He'll do."* One of us was from a silk-weaving village in Fukushima, and had lost her first husband to the flu, and her second to a younger and prettier woman who lived on the other side of the hill, and now she was sailing to America to marry her third. *He's healthy, he doesn't drink, he doesn't gamble, that's all I needed to know.* One of us was a former dancing girl from Nagoya who dressed beautifully, and had translucent white skin, and knew everything there was to know about men, and it was to her we turned every night with our questions. How long will it last? With the lamp lit or in the dark? Legs up or down? Eyes open or closed? What if I can't breathe? What if I get thirsty? What if he is too heavy? What if he is too big? What if he does not want me at all? "Men are really quite simple," she told us. And then she began to explain.

ON THE BOAT we sometimes lay awake for hours in the swaying damp darkness of the hold, filled with longing and dread, and wondered how we would last another three weeks.

ON THE BOAT we carried with us in our trunks all the things we would need for our new lives: white silk kimonos for our wedding night, colorful cotton kimonos for everyday wear, plain cotton kimonos for when we grew old, calligraphy brushes, thick black sticks of ink, thin sheets of rice paper on which to write long letters home, tiny brass Buddhas, ivory statues of the fox god, dolls we had slept with since we were five, bags of brown sugar with which to buy favors, bright cloth quilts, paper fans, English phrase books, flowered silk sashes, smooth black stones from the river that ran behind our house, a lock of hair from a boy we had once touched, and loved, and promised to write, even though we knew we never would, silver mirrors given to us by our mothers, whose last words still rang in our ears. *You will see: women are weak, but mothers are strong.*

ON THE BOAT we complained about everything. Bedbugs. Lice. Insomnia. The constant dull throb of the engine, which worked its way even into our dreams. We complained about the stench from the latrines—huge, gaping holes that opened out onto the sea—and our own slowly ripening odor, which seemed to grow more pungent by the day. We complained about Kazuko's aloofness, Chiyo's throat clearing, Fusayo's incessant humming of the "Teapicker's Song," which was driving us all slowly crazy. We complained about our disappearing hairpins—who among us was the thief?—and how the girls from first class had never once said hello from beneath their violet silk parasols in all the times they had walked past us up above on the deck. *Just who do they think they are?* We complained about the heat. The cold. The scratchy wool blankets. We complained about our own complaining. Deep down, though, most of us were really very happy, for soon we would be in America with our new husbands, who had written to us many times over the months. *I have bought a beautiful house. You can plant tulips in the garden. Daffodils. Whatever you like. I own a farm. I operate a hotel. I am the president of a large bank. I left Japan several years ago to start my own business and can provide for you well. I am 179 centimeters tall and do not suffer from leprosy or lung disease and there is no history of madness in my family. I am a native of Okayama. Of Hyogo. Of Miyagi. Of Shizuoka. I grew up in the village next to*

yours and saw you once years ago at a fair. I will send you the
money for your passage as soon as I can.

ON THE BOAT we carried our husbands' pictures in tiny
oval lockets that hung on long chains from our necks. We
carried them in silk purses and old tea tins and red lacquer
boxes and in the thick brown envelopes from America in
which they had originally been sent. We carried them in
the sleeves of our kimonos, which we touched often, just to
make sure they were still there. We carried them pressed
flat between the pages of *Come, Japanese!* and *Guidance for
Going to America* and *Ten Ways to Please a Man* and old, well-
worn volumes of the Buddhist sutras, and one of us, who
was Christian, and ate meat, and prayed to a different and
longer-haired god, carried hers between the pages of a
King James Bible. And when we asked her which man she
liked better—the man in the photograph or the Lord
Jesus Himself—she smiled mysteriously and replied,
"Him, of course."

SEVERAL OF US on the boat had secrets, which we swore
we would keep from our husbands for the rest of our lives.
Perhaps the real reason we were sailing to America was to
track down a long-lost father who had left the family years
before. *He went to Wyoming to work in the coal mines and we
never heard from him again.* Or perhaps we were leaving
behind a young daughter who had been born to a man
whose face we could now barely recall—a traveling story-
teller who had spent a week in the village, or a wandering
Buddhist priest who had stopped by the house late one

night on his way to Mt. Fuji. And even though we knew our parents would care for her well—*If you stay here in the village,* they had warned us, *you will never marry at all*—we still felt guilty for having chosen our own life over hers, and on the boat we wept for her every night for many nights in a row and then one morning we woke up and dried our eyes and said, "That's enough," and began to think of other things. Which kimono to wear when we landed. How to fix our hair. What to say when we first saw him. Because we were on the boat now, the past was behind us, and there was no going back.

ON THE BOAT we had no idea we would dream of our daughter every night until the day that we died, and that in our dreams she would always be three and as she was when we last saw her: a tiny figure in a dark red kimono squatting at the edge of a puddle, utterly entranced by the sight of a dead floating bee.

ON THE BOAT we ate the same food every day and every day we breathed the same stale air. We sang the same songs and laughed at the same jokes and in the morning, when the weather was mild, we climbed up out of the cramped quarters of the hold and strolled the deck in our wooden sandals and light summer kimonos, stopping, every now and then, to gaze out at the same endless blue sea. Sometimes a flying fish would land at our feet, flopping and out of breath, and one of us—usually it was one of the fishermen's daughters—would pick it up and toss it back into the water. Or a school of dolphins would appear out of nowhere and leap alongside the boat for hours. One calm, windless morning when the sea was flat as glass and the sky a brilliant shade of blue, the smooth black flank of a whale suddenly rose up out of the water and then disappeared and for a moment we forgot to breathe. *It was like looking into the eye of the Buddha.*

ON THE BOAT we often stood on the deck for hours with the wind in our hair, watching the other passengers go by. We saw turbaned Sikhs from the Punjab who were fleeing to Panama from their native land. We saw wealthy White Russians who were fleeing the revolution. We saw Chinese laborers from Hong Kong who were going to work in the cotton fields of Peru. We saw King Lee Uwanowich and his famous band of gypsies, who owned a large cattle ranch in Mexico and were rumored to be the richest band of gypsies in the world. We saw a trio of sunburned German tourists and a handsome Spanish priest and a tall, ruddy Englishman named Charles, who appeared at the railing every afternoon at quarter past three and walked several brisk lengths of the deck. Charles was traveling in first class, and had dark green eyes and a sharp, pointy nose, and spoke perfect Japanese, and was the first white person many of us had ever seen. He was a professor of foreign languages at the university in Osaka, and had a Japanese wife, and a child, and had been to America many times, and was endlessly patient with our questions. Was it true that Americans had a strong animal odor? (Charles laughed and said, "Well, do *I*?" and let us lean in close for a sniff.) And just how hairy *were* they? ("About as hairy as

I am," Charles replied, and then he rolled up his sleeves to show us his arms, which were covered with dark brown hairs that made us shiver.) And did they really grow hair on their chests? (Charles blushed and said he could not show us his chest, and we blushed and explained that we had not asked him to.) And were there still savage tribes of Red Indians wandering all over the prairies? (Charles told us that all the Red Indians had been taken away, and we breathed a sigh of relief.) And was it true that the women in America did not have to kneel down before their husbands or cover their mouths when they laughed? (Charles stared at a passing ship on the horizon and then sighed and said, "Sadly, yes.") And did the men and women there really dance cheek to cheek all night long? (Only on Saturdays, Charles explained.) And were the dance steps very difficult? (Charles said they were easy, and gave us a moonlit lesson on the fox-trot the following evening on the deck. *Slow, slow, quick, quick.*) And was downtown San Francisco truly bigger than the Ginza? (Why, of course.) And were the houses in America really three times the size of our own? (Indeed they were.) And did each house have a piano in the front parlor? (Charles said it was more like every other house.) And did he think we would be happy there? (Charles took off his glasses and looked down at us with his lovely green eyes and said, "Oh yes, very.")

SOME OF US on the boat could not resist becoming friendly with the deckhands, who came from the same villages as we did, and knew all the words to our songs, and were constantly asking us to marry them. We already *are* married, we would explain, but a few of us fell in love with them anyway. And when they asked if they could see us alone—that very same evening, say, on the tween deck, at quarter past ten—we stared down at our feet for a moment and then took a deep breath and said, "Yes," and this was another thing we would never tell our husbands. *It was the way he looked at me,* we would think to ourselves later. Or, *He had a nice smile.*

ONE OF US on the boat became pregnant but did not know it, and when the baby was born nine months later the first thing she would notice was how much it resembled her new husband. *He's got your eyes.* One of us jumped overboard after spending the night with a sailor and left behind a short note on her pillow: *After him, there can be no other.* Another of us fell in love with a returning Methodist missionary she had met on the deck, and even though he begged her to leave her husband for him when they got to America she told him that she could not. "I must remain true to my fate," she said to him. But for the rest of her life she would wonder about the life that could have been.

SOME OF US on the boat were brooders by nature, and preferred to stay to ourselves, and spent most of the voyage lying facedown in our berths, thinking of all the men we had left behind. The fruit seller's son, who always pretended not to notice us but gave us an extra tangerine whenever his mother was not minding the store. Or the married man for whom we had once waited, on a bridge, in the rain, late at night, for two hours. And for what? A kiss and a promise. "I'll come again tomorrow," he'd said. And even though we never saw him again we knew we would do it all over in an instant, because being with him was like being alive for the very first time, only better. And often, as we were falling asleep, we found ourselves thinking of the peasant boy we had talked to every afternoon on our way home from school—the beautiful young boy in the next village whose hands could coax up even the most stubborn of seedlings from the soil—and how our mother, who knew everything, and could often read our mind, had looked at us as though we were crazy. *Do you want to spend the rest of your life crouched over a field?* (We had hesitated, and almost said yes, for hadn't we always dreamed of becoming our mother? Wasn't that all we had ever once wanted to be?)

ON THE BOAT we each had to make choices. Where to sleep and who to trust and who to befriend and how to befriend her. Whether or not to say something to the neighbor who snored, or talked in her sleep, or to the neighbor whose feet smelled even worse than our own, and whose dirty clothes were strewn all over the floor. And if somebody asked us if she looked good when she wore her hair in a certain way—in the "eaves" style, say, which seemed to be taking the boat by storm—and she did not, it made her head look too big, did we tell her the truth, or did we tell her she had never looked better? And was it all right to complain about the cook, who came from China, and only knew how to make one dish—rice curry—which he served to us day after day? But if we said something and he was sent back to China, where on many days you might not get any kind of rice at all, would it then be our fault? And was anybody listening to us anyway? Did anybody care?

SOMEWHERE on the boat there was a captain, from whose cabin a beautiful young girl was said to emerge every morning at dawn. And of course we were all dying to know: Was she one of us, or one of the girls from first class?

ON THE BOAT we sometimes crept into each other's berths late at night and lay quietly side by side, talking about all the things we remembered from home: the smell of roasted sweet potatoes in early autumn, picnics in the bamboo grove, playing shadows and demons in the crumbling temple courtyard, the day our father went out to fetch a bucket of water from the well and did not return, and how our mother never mentioned him even once after that. *It was as though he never even existed. I stared down into that well for years.* We discussed favorite face creams, the benefits of leaden powder, the first time we saw our husband's photograph, what that was like. *He looked like an earnest person, so I figured he was good enough for me.* Sometimes we found ourselves saying things we had never said to anyone, and once we got started it was impossible to stop, and sometimes we grew suddenly silent and lay tangled in each other's arms until dawn, when one of us would pull away from the other and ask, "But will it last?" And that was another choice we had to make. If we said yes, it would last, and went back to her—if not that night, then the next, or the night after that—then we told ourselves that whatever we did would be forgotten the minute we got off the boat. And it was all good practice for our husbands anyway.

A FEW OF US on the boat never did get used to being with a man, and if there had been a way of going to America without marrying one, we would have figured it out.

ON THE BOAT we could not have known that when we first saw our husbands we would have no idea who they were. That the crowd of men in knit caps and shabby black coats waiting for us down below on the dock would bear no resemblance to the handsome young men in the photographs. That the photographs we had been sent were twenty years old. That the letters we had been written had been written to us by people other than our husbands, professional people with beautiful handwriting whose job it was to tell lies and win hearts. That when we first heard our names being called out across the water one of us would cover her eyes and turn away—*I want to go home*—but the rest of us would lower our heads and smooth down the skirts of our kimonos and walk down the gangplank and step out into the still warm day. *This is America,* we would say to ourselves, *there is no need to worry.* And we would be wrong.

FIRST NIGHT

That night our new husbands took us quickly. They took us calmly. They took us gently, but firmly, and without saying a word. They assumed we were the virgins the matchmakers had promised them we were and they took us with exquisite care. *Now let me know if it hurts.* They took us flat on our backs on the bare floor of the Minute Motel. They took us downtown, in second-rate rooms at the Kumamoto Inn. They took us in the best hotels in San Francisco that a yellow man could set foot in at the time. The Kinokuniya Hotel. The Mikado. The Hotel Ogawa. They took us for granted and assumed we would do for them whatever it was we were told. *Please turn toward the wall and drop down on your hands and knees.* They took us by the elbows and said quietly, "It's time." They took us before we were ready and the bleeding did not stop for three days. They took us with our white silk kimonos twisted up high over our heads and we were sure we were about to die. *I thought I was being smothered.* They took us greedily, hungrily, as though they had been waiting to take us for a thousand and one years. They took us even though we were still nauseous from the boat and the ground had not yet stopped rocking beneath our feet. They took us violently, with their fists, whenever we tried

19

to resist. They took us even though we bit them. They took us even though we hit them. They took us even though we insulted them—*You are worth less than the little finger of your mother*—and screamed out for help (nobody came). They took us even though we knelt down at their feet with our foreheads pressed to the ground and pleaded with them to wait. *Can't we do this tomorrow?* They took us by surprise, for some of us had not been told by our mothers exactly what it was that this night would entail. *I was thirteen years old and had never looked a man in the eye.* They took us with apologies for their rough, callused hands, and we knew at once that they were farmers and not bankers. They took us leisurely, from behind, as we leaned out the window to admire the city lights down below. "Are you happy now?" they asked us. They tied us up and took us facedown on threadbare carpets that smelled of mouse droppings and mold. They took us frenziedly, on top of yellow-stained sheets. They took us easily, and with a minimum of fuss, for some of us had been taken many times before. They took us drunkenly. They took us roughly, recklessly, and with no mind for our pain. *I thought my uterus was about to explode.* They took us even though we pressed our legs together and said, "Please, no." They took us cautiously, as though they were afraid we might break. *You're so small.* They took us coldly but knowledgeably—*In twenty seconds you will lose all control*—and we knew there had been many others before us. They took us as we stared up blankly at the ceiling and waited for it to be over, not realizing that it would not be over for years. They took us with the assistance of the innkeeper and his wife, who held us down on the floor to keep us from running away. *No man will want you when he's done.* They took us the way our fathers had taken our mothers every night in the one-room hut back home in the village: suddenly, and without warning, just as we were drifting off into sleep. They took us by lamplight. They took us by moonlight. They took us in darkness, and we could not see a thing. They took us in six seconds and then collapsed on our shoulders with small shuddering sighs, and we thought to ourselves, *That's it?* They took forever, and we knew we would be sore for weeks. They took us on our knees, while we clung to the bedpost and wept. They took us while concentrating fiercely on some mysterious spot on the wall that only they could see. They took us while murmuring "Thank you" over and over again in a familiar Tohoku dialect that immediately set us at ease. *He sounded just like my father.* They took us while shouting out in rough Hiroshima dialects we could barely understand and we knew we were about to spend the rest of our life with a fisherman. They took us upright, in front of the mirror, and made us stare at our reflection the whole time. "You will come to like it," they said to us. They took us politely, by our wrists, and asked us not to scream. They took us shyly, and with great difficulty, as they tried to figure out what to do. "Excuse me," they said. And, "Is this you?" They said, "Help me out here," and so we did. They took us with grunts. They took us with groans. They took us with shouts and long-drawn-out moans. They took us while thinking of some other woman—we could tell by the faraway look in their eyes—and then cursed us afterward when they could find no blood on the sheets. They took us clumsily, and we did not let them touch us again for three years. They took us with more skill than we had ever been taken before and we knew we would always want them. They took us as we cried out with pleasure and then covered our mouths in shame. They took us swiftly, repeatedly, and all throughout the night, and in the morning when we woke we were theirs.

WHITES

We settled on the edges of their towns, when they would let us. And when they would not—*Do not let sundown find you in this county,* their signs sometimes said—we traveled on. We wandered from one labor camp to the next in their hot dusty valleys—the Sacramento, the Imperial, the San Joaquin—and side by side with our new husbands, we worked their land. We picked their strawberries in Watsonville. We picked their grapes in Fresno and Denair. We got down on our knees and dug up their potatoes with garden forks on Bacon Island in the Delta, where the earth was spongy and soft. On the Holland Tract we sorted their green beans. And when the harvest season was over we tied our blanket rolls onto our backs and, cloth bundles in hand, we waited for the next wagon to come, and we traveled on.

THE FIRST WORD of their language we were taught was *water.* Shout it out, our husbands told us, the moment you begin to feel faint in the fields. "Learn this word," they said, "and save your life." Most of us did, but one of us—Yoshiko, who had been raised by wet nurses behind high-walled courtyards in Kobe and had never seen a weed in her life—did not. She went to bed after her first day at the Marble Ranch and she never woke up. "I thought she was sleeping," said her husband. "Heatstroke," the boss explained. Another of us was too shy to shout and knelt down and drank from an irrigation ditch instead. Seven days later she was burning up with typhoid. Other words we soon learned: "All right"—what the boss said when he was satisfied with our work—and "Go home"—what he said when we were too clumsy or slow.

HOME WAS A COT in one of their bunkhouses at the Fair Ranch in Yolo. Home was a long tent beneath a leafy plum tree at Kettleman's. Home was a wooden shanty in Camp No. 7 on the Barnhart Tract out in Lodi. *Nothing but rows of onions as far as the eye can see.* Home was a bed of straw in John Lyman's barn alongside his prize horses and cows. Home was a corner of the washhouse at Stockton's Cannery Ranch. Home was a bunk in a rusty boxcar in Lompoc. Home was an old chicken coop in Willows that the Chinese had lived in before us. Home was a flea-ridden mattress in a corner of a packing shed in Dixon. Home was a bed of hay atop three apple crates beneath an apple tree in Fred Stadelman's apple orchard. Home was a spot on the floor of an abandoned schoolhouse in Marysville. Home was a patch of earth in a pear orchard in Auburn not far from the banks of the American River, where we lay awake every evening staring up at the American stars, which looked no different from ours: there, up above us, was the Cowherd Star, the Weaver Maiden Star, the Wood

Star, the Water Star. "Same latitude," our husbands explained. Home was wherever the crops were ripe and ready for picking. Home was wherever our husbands were. Home was by the side of a man who had been shoveling up weeds for the boss for years.

IN THE BEGINNING we wondered about them constantly. Why did they mount their horses from the left side and not the right? How were they able to tell each other apart? Why were they always shouting? Did they really hang dishes on their walls and not pictures? And have locks on all their doors? And wear their shoes inside the house? What did they talk about late at night as they were falling asleep? What did they dream of? To whom did they pray? How many gods did they have? Was it true that they really saw a man in the moon and not a rabbit? And ate cooked beef at funerals? And drank the milk of cows? And that smell? What was it? "Butter stink," our husbands explained.

STAY AWAY FROM THEM, we were warned. Approach them with caution, if you must. Do not always believe what they tell you, but learn to watch them closely: their hands, their eyes, the corners of their mouths, sudden changes in the color of their skin. You will soon be able to read them. Make sure, however, that you don't stare. With time you will grow accustomed to their largeness. Expect the worst, but do not be surprised by moments of kindness. There is goodness all around. Remember to make them feel comfortable. Be humble. Be polite. Appear eager to please. Say "Yes, sir," or "No, sir," and do as you're told. Better yet, say nothing at all. You now belong to the invisible world.

THEIR PLOWS WEIGHED more than we did, and were difficult to use, and their horses were twice the size of our horses back home in Japan. We could not harness them without climbing up onto orange crates, or standing on stools, and the first time we shouted out to them to move they just stood there snorting and pawing at the ground. Were they deaf? Were they dumb? Or were they just being stubborn? "These are American horses," our husbands explained. "They don't understand Japanese." And so we learned our first words of horse English. "Giddyap" was what you said to make the horse go forward, and "Back" was what you said to make it back up. "Easy" was what you said to make it slow down, and "Whoa" was what you said to make it stop. And after fifty years in America these would be the only words of English some of us could still remember by heart.

WE HAD LEARNED a few phrases of their language on the boat from our guidebooks—"Hello," "Beg pardon," "Please pay me my wages"—and could recite their ABCs, but in America this knowledge was useless. We could not read their magazines or newspapers. We stared at their signs in despair. *All I remember is it began with the letter* e. And whenever the boss spoke to us we could hear his words perfectly clearly but they made no sense to our ears. And on the rare occasions when we had to make ourselves known to them—*Mr. Smeesh?*—they stared at us in bewilderment, then shrugged their shoulders and walked away.

DON'T LET THEM *discourage you. Be patient. Stay calm. But for now,* our husbands told us, *please leave the talking to me.* For they already spoke the English language. They understood the American ways. And whenever we needed new underwear they swallowed their pride and walked through the hot blazing fields into town and in perfect but heavily accented English they asked the shopkeeper for a new pair. "Not for me," they explained. And when we arrived at a new ranch and the boss took one look at us and said, "She's too frail," it was our husbands who convinced him otherwise. "In the fields my wife is as good as a man," they would say, and in no time at all this was true. And when we fell ill with malaria and could not lift our heads off the floor it was our husbands who told the boss what was wrong: "First she's hot, then she's cold, then she's hot again." And when the boss himself offered to drive into town that very same afternoon to buy us the medicine that would cure us—"Don't you worry about the money," he said—it was our husbands who thanked him profusely. And even though that medicine turned our urine dark purple for days, we soon began to feel well.

SOME OF US worked quickly to impress them. Some of us worked quickly just to show them that we could pick plums and top beets and sack onions and crate berries just as quickly if not more quickly than the men. Some of us worked quickly because we had spent our entire child-hoods bent over barefoot in the rice paddies and already knew what to do. Some of us worked quickly because our husbands had warned us that if we did not they would send us home on the very next boat. *I asked for a wife who was able and strong.* Some of us came from the city, and worked slowly, because we had never before held a hoe. "Easiest job in America," we were told. Some of us had been sickly and weak all our lives but after one week in the lemon groves of Riverside we felt stronger than oxen. One of us collapsed before she had even finished weeding her first row. Some of us wept while we worked. Some of us cursed while we worked. All of us ached while we worked—our hands blistered and bled, our knees burned, our backs would never recover. One of us was distracted by the handsome Hindu man cutting asparagus in the next fur-row over while she worked and all she could think of was how much she wanted to unravel his white turban from his enormous brown head. *I dream about Gupta-san nightly.* Some of us chanted Buddhist sutras while we worked and the hours flew by like minutes. One of us—Akiko, who had gone to a mission school in Tokyo and already knew English and read aloud to her husband every night from the Bible—sang "Arise, My Soul, Arise" while she worked. Many more of us sang the same harvest songs we had sung in our youth and tried to imagine we were back home in Japan. Because if our husbands had told us the truth in their letters—they were not silk traders, they were fruit pickers, they did not live in large, many-roomed houses, they lived in tents and in barns and out of doors, in the fields, beneath the sun and the stars—we never would have come to America to do the work that no self-respecting American would do.

THEY ADMIRED US for our strong backs and nimble hands. Our stamina. Our discipline. Our docile dispositions. Our unusual ability to tolerate the heat, which on summer days in the melon fields of Brawley could reach 120 degrees. They said that our short stature made us ideally suited for work that required stooping low to the ground. Wherever they put us they were pleased. We had all the virtues of the Chinese—we were hardworking, we were patient, we were unfailingly polite—but none of their vices—we didn't gamble or smoke opium, we didn't brawl, we never spat. We were faster than the Filipinos and less arrogant than the Hindus. We were more disciplined than the Koreans. We were soberer than the Mexicans. We were cheaper to feed than the Okies and Arkies, both the light and the dark. *A Japanese can live on a teaspoonful of rice a day.* We were the best breed of worker they had ever hired in their lives. *These folks just drift, we don't have to look after them at all.*

BY DAY we worked in their orchards and fields but every night, while we slept, we returned home. Sometimes we dreamed we were back in the village, rolling a metal hoop down the Street of Rich Merchants with our favorite forked wooden stick. Other times we were playing hide-and-seek in the reeds down by the river. And every once in a while we'd see something float by. A red silk ribbon we'd lost years before. A speckled blue egg. Our mother's wooden pillow. A turtle that had wandered away from us when we were four. Sometimes we were standing in front of the mirror with our older sister, Ai, whose name meant either "love" or "grief," depending on how you wrote it, and she was braiding our hair. "Stand still!" she said. And everything was as it should be. But when we woke up we found ourselves lying beside a strange man in a strange land in a hot crowded shed that was filled with the grunts and sighs of others. Sometimes that man reached out for us in his sleep with his thick, gnarled hands and we tried not to pull away. *In ten years he will be an old man,* we told ourselves. Sometimes he opened his eyes in the early dawn light and saw that we were sad, and he promised us that things would get better. And even though we had said to him only hours before, "I detest you," as he climbed on top of us once more in the darkness, we let ourselves be comforted, for he was all that we had. Sometimes he looked right through us without seeing us at all, and that was always the worst. *Does anyone even know I am here?*

ALL WEEK LONG they made us sweat for them in the fields but on Sundays, they let us rest. And while our husbands wandered into town and played fan-tan at the local Chinese gambling hall, where the house always won, we sat down beneath the trees with our inkstones and brushes and on long, thin sheets of rice paper we wrote home to our mothers, whom we had promised never to leave. *We are in America now, picking weeds for the big man they call Boss. There are no mulberry trees here, no bamboo groves, no statues of Jizo by the side of the road. The hills are brown and dry and the rain rarely falls. The mountains are far away. We live by the light of oil lamps and once a week, on Sundays, we wash our clothes on wet stones in the stream. My husband is not the man in the photograph. My husband is the man in the photograph but aged by many years. My husband's handsome best friend is the man in the photograph. My husband is a drunkard. My husband is the manager of the Yamato Club and his entire torso is covered with tattoos. My husband is shorter than he claimed to be in his letters, but then again, so am I. My husband was awarded the Sixth Class Order of the Golden Kite during the Russo-Japanese War and now walks with a pronounced limp. My husband was smuggled into the country across the Mexican border. My husband is a stowaway who jumped ship in San Francisco the day before the great earthquake of 1906 and every night he dreams he must get to the ferry. My husband adores me. My husband will not leave me alone. My husband is a good man who works extra hard whenever I cannot keep up the pace so the boss does not send me home.*

SECRETLY, we hoped to be rescued from them. Perhaps we had fallen in love with a man on the boat who came from the same island as we did, and remembered the same mountains and streams, and we could not get him out of our mind. Every day he had stood beside us on the deck and told us how pretty we were, how clever, how *special*. He'd never met anyone like us in his life, he'd said. He'd said, "Wait for me. I will send for you as soon as I can." Perhaps he was a labor contractor in Cortez, or the president of an import-export company in downtown San Jose, and every day as we dug down into the black, sun-baked earth with our hands we prayed that a letter from him would arrive. And every day there was nothing. Sometimes, late at night, as we were getting ready for bed, we suddenly burst into tears and our husband would look at us with concern. "Was it something I said?" he would ask, and we would just shake our heads no. But when the envelope from the man on the boat finally did arrive one day in the mail—*I have sent money to your husband and will be waiting for you at the Taisho Hotel*—we had to tell our husband everything. And even though he struck us many times with his belt and called us many well-deserved names, in the end he let us go. Because the money he received from the man on the boat was several times the amount he had spent to bring us over from Japan. "At least now maybe one of us will be happy," he said to us. He said, "Nothing lasts for long." He said, "The first time I looked into your eyes I should have known they were the eyes of a whore."

SOMETIMES the boss would approach us from behind while we were bending over his fields and whisper a few words into our ears. And even though we had no idea what he was saying we knew exactly what he meant. "Me no speak English," we'd reply. Or, "So sorry, Boss, but no." Sometimes we were approached by a well-dressed fellow countryman who appeared out of nowhere and offered to take us back with him to the big city. *If you come work for me I can pay you ten times what you earn in the fields.* Sometimes one of our husband's unmarried worker friends approached us the moment our husband stepped away and tried to slip us a five-dollar bill. "Just let me put it in once," he'd say to us. "I promise you I won't even move it." And every now and then we'd give in and say yes. "Meet me tomorrow night behind the lettuce shed at nine," we'd tell him. Or, "For five dollars more I'll do it." Perhaps we were unhappy with our husband, who went out to play cards and drink every night and did not come home until late. Or perhaps we needed to send money to our family back home because their rice fields had once again been ruined by floods. *We have lost everything and are living on nothing but tree bark and boiled yams.* Even those of us who were not pretty were often offered gifts on the sly: a tortoiseshell hairpin, a bottle of perfume, a copy of *Modern Screen* magazine that had been stolen from the counter of a dime store in town. But if we accepted that gift without giving anything back in return we knew there would be a price to pay. *He sliced off the tip of her finger with his pruning knife.* And so we learned to think twice before saying yes and looking into another man's eyes, because in America you got nothing for free.

SOME OF US worked as cooks in their labor camps, and some of us as dishwashers, and ruined our delicate hands. Others of us were brought out to their remote interior valleys to work as sharecroppers on their land. Perhaps our husband had rented twenty acres from a man named Caldwell, who owned thousands of acres in the heart of the southern San Joaquin Valley, and every year we paid Mr. Caldwell sixty percent of our yield. We lived in a dirt-floored shack beneath a willow tree in the middle of a wide, open field and slept on a mattress stuffed with straw. We relieved ourselves outside, in a hole in the ground. We drew our water up from a well. We spent our days planting and picking tomatoes from dawn until dusk and spoke to no one but our husband for weeks at a time. We had a cat to keep us company, and chase away the rats, and at night if we stood in the doorway and looked out toward the west we could see a faint, flickering light in the distance. That, our husband had told us, was where people were. And we knew we never should have left home. But no matter how loudly we called out for our mother we knew she could not hear us, so we tried to make the best of what we had. We cut out pictures of cakes from magazines and hung them on the walls. We sewed curtains out of bleached rice sacks. We made Buddhist altars out of overturned tomato crates that we covered with cloth, and every morning we left out a cup of hot tea for our ancestors. And at the end of the harvest season we walked ten miles into town and bought ourselves a small gift: a bottle of Coke, a new apron, a tube of lipstick, which we might one day have occasion to wear. *Perhaps I shall be invited to a concert.* Some years our crops were good and the prices were high and we made more money than we'd ever dreamed of. *Six hundred an acre.* Other years we lost everything to insects or mildew or a month of heavy rains, or the price of tomatoes fell so low that we had no choice but to auction off all our tools to pay off our debts, and we wondered why we were there. "I was a fool to follow you out into the country," we said to our husband. Or, "You are wasting my youth." But when he asked us if we would rather be working as a maid in the city, smiling and bowing and saying nothing but "Yes, ma'am, yes, ma'am," all day long, we had to admit that the answer was no.

THEY DID NOT want us as neighbors in their valleys. They did not want us as friends. We lived in unsightly shacks and could not speak plain English. We cared only about money. Our farming methods were poor. We used too much water. We did not plow deeply enough. Our husbands worked us like slaves. *They import those girls from Japan as free labor.* We worked in the fields all day long without stopping for supper. We worked in the fields late at night by the light of our kerosene lamps. We never took a single day off. *A clock and a bed are two things a Japanese farmer never used in his life.* We were taking over their cauliflower industry. We had taken over their spinach industry. We had a monopoly on their strawberry industry and had cornered their market on beans. We were an unbeatable, unstoppable economic machine and if our progress was not checked the entire western United States would soon become the next Asiatic outpost and colony.

MANY NIGHTS, we waited for them. Sometimes they drove by our farm shacks and sprayed our windows with buckshot, or set our chicken coops on fire. Sometimes they dynamited our packing sheds. Sometimes they burned down our fields just as they were beginning to ripen and we lost our entire earnings for that year. And even though we found footsteps in the dirt the following morning, and many scattered matchsticks, when we called the sheriff to come out and take a look he told us there were no clues worth following. And after that our husbands were never the same. *Why even bother?* At night we slept with our shoes on, and hatchets beside our beds, while our husbands sat by the windows until dawn. Sometimes we were startled awake by a sound but it was nothing—somewhere in the world, perhaps, a peach had just dropped from a tree— and sometimes we slept straight through the night and in the morning when we woke we found our husbands slumped over and snoring in their chairs and we tried to wake them gently, for their rifles were still resting on their laps. Sometimes our husbands bought themselves guard dogs, which they named Dick or Harry or Spot, and they grew more attached to those dogs than they ever did to us, and we wondered if we had made a mistake, coming to such a violent and unwelcoming land. *Is there any tribe more savage than the Americans?*

ONE OF US blamed them for everything and wished that they were dead. One of us blamed them for everything and wished that she were dead. Others of us learned to live without thinking of them at all. We threw ourselves into our work and became obsessed with the thought of pulling one more weed. We put away our mirrors. We stopped combing our hair. We forgot about makeup. *Whenever I powder my nose it just looks like frost on a mountain.* We forgot about Buddha. We forgot about God. We developed a coldness inside us that still has not thawed. *I fear my soul has died.* We stopped writing home to our mothers. We lost weight and grew thin. We stopped bleeding. We stopped dreaming. We stopped wanting. We simply worked, that was all. We gulped down our meals three times a day without saying a word to our husbands so we could hurry back out into the fields. *"One minute sooner to pull one more weed." I could not get this thought out of my mind.* We spread our legs for them every evening but were so exhausted we often fell asleep before they were done. We washed their clothes for them once a week in tubs of boiling hot water. We cooked for them. We cleaned for them. We helped them chop wood. But it was not we who were cooking and cleaning and chopping, it was somebody else. And often our husbands did not even notice we'd disappeared.

SOME OF US moved out of the countryside and into their suburbs and got to know them well. We lived in the servants' quarters of the big houses in Atherton and Berkeley, above Telegraph, up high in the hills. Or we worked for a man like Dr. Giordano, who was a prominent thoracic surgeon on Alameda's gold coast. And while our husband mowed Dr. Giordano's lawn and pruned Dr. Giordano's shrubs and raked Dr. Giordano's leaves, we stayed inside with Mrs. Giordano, who had wavy brown hair and a kind manner and asked us to please call her Rose, and we polished Rose's silver and we swept Rose's floors and we tended to Rose's three young children, Richard, Jim, and Theo, whom we sang to sleep every night in a language not their own. *Nemure, nemure.* And it was not at all what we had expected. *I have come to care for those boys as though they were my own.* But it was Dr. Giordano's elderly mother, Lucia, whom we came to care for the most. Lucia was even lonelier than we were, and almost as short, and once she overcame her fear of us she never left our side. She followed us from one room to the next as we dusted and mopped and not once did she ever stop talking. *Molto bene. Perfetto! Basta così.* And for many years after her death her memories of the old country would continue to linger with us as though they were our own: the mozzarella, the *pomodori,* the Lago di Como, the piazza in the center of town where she went shopping with her sisters every day. *Italia, Italia, how I long to see it one last time.*

IT WAS THEIR WOMEN who taught us the things we most needed to know. How to light a stove. How to make a bed. How to answer a door. How to shake a hand. How to operate a faucet, which many of us had never seen in our lives. How to dial a telephone. How to sound cheerful on a telephone even when you were angry or sad. How to fry an egg. How to peel a potato. How to set a table. How to prepare a five-course dinner in six hours for a party of twelve. How to light a cigarette. How to blow a smoke ring. How to curl your hair so it looked just like Mary Pickford's. How to wash a lipstick stain out of your husband's favorite white shirt even when that lipstick stain was not yours. How to raise up your skirt on the street to reveal just the right amount of ankle. *You must aim to tantalize, not tease.* How to talk to a husband. How to argue with a husband. How to deceive a husband. How to keep a husband from wandering too far from your side. *Don't ask him where he's been or what time he'll be coming home and make sure he is happy in bed.*

WE LOVED THEM. We hated them. We wanted to *be* them. How tall they were, how lovely, how fair. Their long, graceful limbs. Their bright white teeth. Their pale, luminous skin, which disguised all seven blemishes of the face. Their odd but endearing ways, which never ceased to amuse—their love of A.1. sauce and high, pointy-toed shoes, their funny, turned-out walk, their tendency to gather in each other's parlors in large, noisy groups and stand around talking, all at once, for hours. Why, we wondered, did it never occur to them to sit down? They seemed so at home in the world. So at ease. They had a confidence that we lacked. And much better hair. *So many colors.* And we regretted that we could not be more like them.

LATE AT NIGHT, in our narrow, windowless rooms in the backs of their large, stately houses, we imitated them. "Now you be the master and I'll be the missus," we said to our husbands. "No, *you* be the master and *I'll* be the missus," they sometimes replied. We tried to imagine how they did it. What they said. Who was on top. Who was on the bottom. Did he cry out? Did she? Did they wake up in the morning with their limbs intertwined? Other times we lay quietly in the darkness and told each other about our days. *I beat the rugs. I boiled the sheets. I dug up the devil grass with my farmer's knife from the south side of the lawn.* And when we were finished we pulled up the covers and closed our eyes and dreamed of better times to come. A pretty white house of our own on a long, shady street with a garden that was always in bloom. A bathtub that filled up with hot water in mere minutes. A servant who brought us breakfast every morning on a round silver tray and swept all the rooms by hand. A chambermaid. A laundress. A Chinese butler in a long white coat who appeared the moment we rang a bell and called out, "Charlie, please bring me my tea!"

THEY GAVE US new names. They called us Helen and Lily. They called us Margaret. They called us Pearl. They marveled at our tiny figures and our long, shiny black hair. They praised us for our hardworking ways. *That girl never stops until she gets the job done.* They bragged about us to their neighbors. They bragged about us to their friends. They claimed to like us much more than they did any of the others. *No better class of help can be found.* When they were unhappy and had no one to talk to they told us their deep, darkest secrets. *Everything I told him was a lie.* When their husbands went away on business they asked us to sleep with them in their bedrooms in case they got lonely. When they called out for us in the middle of the night we went to them and lay with them until morning. "Hush, hush," we said to them. And, "Please don't cry." When they fell in love with a man who was not their husband we kept an eye on their children while they went out to meet that man in the middle of the day. "Do I look all right?" they asked us. And, "Is my skirt too tight?" We brushed off invisible specks of lint from their blouses, retied scarves, adjusted stray locks of hair so they hung just so. We plucked out their grays without comment. "You look beautiful," we said to them, and then we sent them on their way. And when their husbands came home in the evening at the usual hour we pretended not to know a thing.

ONE OF THEM lived alone in a run-down mansion on top of San Francisco's Nob Hill and had not been outside in twelve years. One of them was a countess from Dresden who had never lifted up anything heavier than a fork. One of them had fled from the Bolsheviks in Russia and every night she dreamed she was back in her father's house in Odessa. *We lost it all.* One of them had used only Negroes before us. One of them had had bad luck with the Chinese. *You have to keep an eye on them all the time.* One of them made us get down on our hands and knees every time we scrubbed her floor instead of using a mop. One of them grabbed a rag and tried to help us but only ended up getting in our way. One of them served us elaborate lunches on fine china plates and insisted that we sit down with her at the table, even though we were anxious to get on with our work. One of them never changed out of her nightgown until noon. Several of them suffered from headaches. Many of them were sad. Most drank. One of them took us downtown to the City of Paris department store every Friday afternoon and told us to pick out a new item of clothing. *Whatever you like.* One of them gave us a dictionary and a pair of white silk gloves and enrolled us in our first class in English. *My driver will be waiting for you downstairs.* Others tried to teach us themselves. *This is a bucket. This is a mop. This is a broom.* One of them could never remember our name. One of them greeted us warmly every morning in the kitchen but whenever she passed us outside on the street she had no idea who we were. One of them barely said a word to us in the thirteen years that we worked for her but when she died she left us a fortune.

WE LIKED IT BEST when they were out having their hair done, or eating lunch at the club, and their husbands were still away at the office, and their children not yet home from school. Nobody was watching us then. Nobody was talking to us. Nobody was sneaking up on us from behind as we were cleaning her fixtures to see if we'd missed any spots. The whole house was empty. Quiet. Ours. We pulled back curtains. Opened windows. Breathed in the fresh air as we moved from one room to the next, dusting and polishing their things. *All they see is the shine.* We felt calmer then. Less afraid. We felt, for once, like ourselves.

A FEW OF US stole from them. Little things, at first, which we did not think they would miss. A silver fork here. A saltshaker there. The occasional swig of brandy. A beautiful rose-patterned teacup we just had to have. A beautiful rose-patterned saucer. A porcelain vase that was the same shade of green as our mother's jade Buddha. *I just like pretty things.* A handful of change that had been sitting out on the counter for days. Others of us, though tempted, kept our hands to ourselves, and for our honesty we were well rewarded. *I'm the only servant she'll let upstairs in her bedroom. All the Negroes have to stay down below in the kitchen.*

SOME OF THEM dismissed us without any warning and we had no idea what it was we'd done wrong. "You were too pretty," our husbands would tell us, even though we found it hard to believe this was true. Some of us were so inept we knew we would not last more than one week. We forgot to cook their meat before serving it to them for supper. We burned their oatmeal every time. We dropped their best crystal goblets. We threw out their cheese by mistake. "I thought it was rotten," we tried to explain. "That's how it's *supposed* to smell," we were told. Some of us had trouble understanding their English, which bore no resemblance to what we had learned in our books. We said "Yes" when they asked us if we would mind folding their laundry and "No" when they asked us to mop, and when they asked us if we'd seen their missing gold earrings we smiled and said, "Oh, is that so?" Others of us just answered "Um-hmm" to whatever they said. Some of us had husbands who had lied to them about our abilities in the kitchen—*My wife's specialties are chicken Kiev and vichyssoise*—but it soon became apparent that our only specialty was rice. Some of us had grown up on large estates with servants of our own and could not tolerate being told what to do. Some of us did not get along well with their children, whom we found aggressive and loud. Some of us objected to what they said about us to their children when they did not realize we were still in the room. *If you don't study harder, you'll end up scrubbing floors just like Lily.*

MOST OF THEM took little notice of us at all. We were there when they needed us and when they did not, poof, we were gone. We stayed in the background, quietly mopping their floors, waxing their furniture, bathing their children, cleaning the parts of their houses that nobody but us could see. We spoke seldom. We ate little. We were gentle. We were good. We never caused any trouble and allowed them to do with us as they pleased. We let them praise us when they were happy with us. We let them yell at us when they were mad. We let them give us things we did not really want, or need. *If I don't take that old sweater she'll accuse me of being too proud.* We did not bother them with questions. We never talked back or complained. We never asked for a raise. For most of us were simple girls from the country who did not speak any English and in America we knew we had no choice but to scrub sinks and wash floors.

WE DID NOT mention them in our letters to our mothers. We did not mention them in our letters to our sisters or friends. Because in Japan the lowliest job a woman could have was that of a maid. *We have quit the fields and moved into a nice house in town, where my husband has found employment with a family of the first rank. I am putting on weight. I've blossomed. I've grown half an inch. I wear underwear now. I wear a corset and stockings. I wear a white cotton brassiere. I sleep in until nine every morning and spend my afternoons out of doors with the cat in the garden. My face is fuller. My hips have widened. My stride has lengthened. I am learning how to read. I am taking piano lessons. I have mastered the art of American baking and recently won first prize in a contest for my lemon meringue pie. I know you would like it here. The streets are wide and clean and you do not have to take off your shoes when you walk on the grass. I think of you often and will send money home as soon as I can.*

FROM TIME TO TIME one of their men would ask to have a word with us in his study while his wife was out shopping, and we did not know how to say no. "Is everything all right?" he would ask us. Usually we stared down at the floor and said yes, of course, everything was fine, even though this was not true, but when he touched us lightly on the shoulder and asked us if we were sure, we did not always turn away. "Nobody has to know," he would say to us. Or, "She's not due home until late." And when he led us upstairs to the bedroom and laid us across the bed—the very same bed we had made up that morning—we wept because it had been so long since we'd been held.

SOME OF THEM asked us to speak a few words in Japanese for them just to hear the sound of our voice. *It doesn't matter what you say.* Some of them asked us to put on our finest silk kimonos for them and walk slowly up and down their spines. Some of them asked us to tie them up with our flowered silk sashes and call them whatever names came to mind, and we were surprised at what those names were, and how easily they came to us, for we had never before said them out loud. Some of them asked us to tell them our real names, which they then whispered to us again and again until we no longer knew who we were. *Midori. Midori. Midori.* Some of them told us how beautiful we were, even though we knew we were homely and plain. *No man would look at me in Japan.* Some of them asked us how we liked it, or if they were hurting us, and if so were we enjoying the pain, and we said yes, for we were. *At least when I'm with you I know I'm alive.* Some of them lied to us. *I've never done this before.* And we, in turn, lied to them. *Neither have I.* Some of them gave us money, which we slipped into our stockings and gave to our husbands that same evening without saying a word. Some of them promised to leave their wives for us, even though we knew they never would. Some of them found out we were pregnant by them—*My husband has not touched me in more than six months*—and then sent us away. "You must get rid of it," they said to us. They said, "I will pay for everything."

They said, "I will find you employment elsewhere at once."

ONE OF US made the mistake of falling in love with him and still thinks of him night and day. One of us confessed everything to her husband, who beat her with a broom-stick and then lay down and wept. One of us confessed everything to her husband, who divorced her and sent her back to her parents in Japan, where she now works in a silk-reeling mill in Nagano for ten hours a day. One of us confessed everything to her husband, who forgave her and then confessed to a few sins of his own. *I have a second fam-ily up in Colusa.* One of us said nothing to anyone and slowly lost her mind. One of us wrote home for advice to her mother, who always knew what to do, but never received a reply. *I must cross this bridge by myself.* One of us filled the sleeves of her white silk wedding kimono with stones and wandered out into the sea, and we still say a prayer for her every day.

A FEW OF US ended up servicing them exclusively in pink hotels above pool halls and liquor stores in the seed-ier parts of their towns. We shouted out to them from the second-story windows of the Tokyo House, where the youngest of us was barely ten years old. We gazed at them over the tops of our painted paper fans at the Yokohama House, and for the right price we did for them whatever their wives would not do for them at home. We introduced ourselves to them as Mistress Saki and Honorable Miss

Cherry Blossom in high, girlish voices at the Aloha House, and when they asked us where we were from we smiled and said, "Oh, somewhere in Kyoto." We danced with them at the New Eden Night Club and charged them fifty cents for every fifteen minutes of our time. And if they wanted to come upstairs with us we told them it was five dollars a go, or twenty dollars to keep the room until morning. And when they were finished with us we handed their money over to our bosses, who gambled nightly, and paid regular bribes to the police, and would not let us sleep with anyone of our own race. *A pretty girl like you is worth a thousand pieces of gold.*

SOMETIMES, while we were lying with them, we found ourselves longing for our husbands, from whom we had run away. *Was he really so bad? So brutal? So dull?* Sometimes we found ourselves falling in love with our bosses, who had kidnapped us at knifepoint as we were coming in from the fields. *He brings me things. He talks to me. He lets me go for walks.* Sometimes we convinced ourselves that after one year at the Eureka House we would have enough money to pay for our passage back home, but at the end of that year all we had was fifty cents and a bad dose of the clap. *Next year,* we told ourselves. *Or maybe the year after that.* But even the prettiest of us knew that our days were numbered, for in our line of work you were either finished or dead by the time you were twenty.

ONE OF THEM bought us out of the brothel where we worked and brought us home to a big house on a tree-lined street in Montecito, whose name we shall not reveal. There were hibiscus in the windows, marble tabletops, leather sofas, glass dishes filled with nuts for whenever the guests stopped by. There was a beloved white dog we named Shiro, after the dog we had left behind in Japan, and we walked her with pleasure three times a day. There was an electric icebox. A Gramophone. A Majestic radio. A Model T Ford in the driveway that we cranked up every Sunday and took out for a drive. There was a tiny maid named Consuelo, who came from the Philippines, and baked wonderful custards, and pies, and anticipated our every need. She knew when we were happy. She knew when we were sad. She knew when we'd fought the night before and when we'd had a good time. And for all of this we were forever grateful to our new husband, without whom we would still be working the streets. *The moment I saw him I knew I'd been saved.* But every now and then we'd find ourselves wondering about the man we had left behind. Did he burn all our things the day after we left him? Did he tear up our letters? Did he hate us? Did he miss us? Did he care whether we were dead or alive? Was he still working as a yardman for the Burnhams on Sutter Street? Had he put in their daffodils yet? Had he finished reseeding their lawn? Did he still eat his supper alone, every evening, in Mrs. Burnham's great big kitchen, or had he finally made friends with Mrs. Burnham's favorite Negro maid? Did he still read three pages from the *Manual of Gardening* every night before going to bed? Did he still dream of one day becoming majordomo? Sometimes, in the late afternoon, just as the light was beginning to fade, we took out his yellowing photograph from our trunk and looked at it one last time. But no matter how hard we tried we could not make ourselves throw it away.

A NUMBER OF US found ourselves hunched over their galvanized tin washtubs on our third day in America, quietly scrubbing their things: stained pillowcases and bedsheets, soiled handkerchiefs, dirty collars, white lace slips so lovely we thought they should be worn over, and not under. We worked in basement laundries in Japantowns in the most run-down sections of their cities—San Francisco, Sacramento, Santa Barbara, L.A.—and every morning we rose before dawn with our husbands and we washed and we boiled and we scrubbed. And at night when we put down our brushes and climbed into bed we dreamed we were still washing, as we would every night for years. And even though we had not come all the way to America to live in a tiny, curtained-off room at the back of the Royal Hand Laundry, we knew we could not go home. *If you come home,* our fathers had written to us, *you will disgrace the entire family. If you come home your younger sisters will never marry. If you come home no man will ever have you again.* And so we stayed in J-town with our new husbands, and grew old before our time.

IN J-TOWN we rarely saw them at all. We waited tables seven days a week at our husbands' lunch counters and noodle shops, where we knew all the regulars by heart. Yamamoto-san. Natsuhara-san. Eto-san, Kodami-san. We cleaned the rooms of our husbands' cheap boarding-houses, and twice a day we cooked meals for their guests, who looked just like ourselves. We bought our groceries at Fujioka Grocery, where they sold all the things we remembered from home: green leaf tea, Mitsuwa soap, incense, pickled plums, fresh tofu, dried seaweed to help fend off goiters and cold. We bought bootleg sake for our husbands at the pool hall beneath the brothel on the corner of Third and Main, but made sure to put on our white aprons first so we would not be mistaken for whores in the alley. We bought our dresses at Yada Ladies' Shop and our shoes at Asahi Shoe, where the shoes actually came in our size. We bought our face cream at Tenshodo Drug. We went to the public bathhouse every Saturday and gossiped with our neighbors and friends. Was it true that Kisayo refused to let her husband enter the house through the front door? Had Mikiko really run away with a card dealer from the Toyo Club? And what had Hagino done to her hair? *It looks like a rat's nest.* We went to Yoshinaga's Dental Clinic for our toothaches, and for our back and knee pains we went to Dr. Hayano, the acupuncturist, who also knew the art of shiatsu massage. And whenever we needed advice in matters of the heart—*Should I leave him or should I stay?*—we went to Mrs. Murata, the fortune-teller, who lived in the blue house on Second Street above Asakawa Pawn, and we sat with her in her kitchen with our heads bowed and our hands on our knees while we waited for her to receive a message from the gods. *If you leave him now there will be no other.* And all of this took place on a four-block-long stretch of town that was more Japanese than the village we'd left behind in Japan. *If I close my eyes I don't even know I'm living in a foreign land.*

WHENEVER WE LEFT J-town and wandered through the broad, clean streets of their cities we tried not to draw attention to ourselves. We dressed like they did. We walked like they did. We made sure not to travel in large groups. We made ourselves small for them—*If you stay in your place they'll leave you alone*—and did our best not to offend. Still, they gave us a hard time. Their men slapped our husbands on the back and shouted out, "So solly!" as they knocked off our husbands' hats. Their children threw stones at us. Their waiters always served us last. Their ushers led us upstairs, to the second balconies of their theaters, and seated us in the worst seats in the house. *Nigger heaven,* they called it. Their barbers refused to cut our hair. *Too coarse for our scissors.* Their women asked us to move away from them in their trolley cars whenever we were standing too close. "Please excuse," we said to them, and then we smiled and stepped aside. Because the only way to resist, our husbands had taught us, was by not resisting. Mostly, though, we stayed at home, in J-town, where we felt safe among our own. We learned to live at a distance from them, and avoided them whenever we could.

ONE DAY, we promised ourselves, we would leave them. We would work hard and save up enough money to go to some other place. Argentina, perhaps. Or Mexico. Or São

Paulo, Brazil. Or Harbin, Manchuria, where our husbands had told us a Japanese could live like a prince. *My brother went there last year and made a killing.* We would start all over again. Open our own fruit stand. Our own trading company. Our own first-class hotel. We'd plant a cherry orchard. A persimmon grove. Buy a thousand acres of rich golden field. We would learn things. Do things. Build an orphanage. Build a temple. Take our first ride on a train. And once a year, on our anniversary, we'd put on our lipstick and go out to eat. *Someplace fancy, with white tablecloths and chandeliers.* And when we'd saved up enough money to help our parents live a more comfortable life we would pack up our things and go back home to Japan. It would be autumn, and our fathers would be out threshing in the fields. We would walk through the mulberry groves, past the big loquat tree and the old lotus pond, where we used to catch tadpoles in spring. Our dogs would come running up to us. Our neighbors would wave. Our mothers would be sitting by the well with their sleeves tied up, washing the evening's rice. And when they saw us they would just stand up and stare. "Little girl," they would say to us, "where in the world have you been?"

BUT UNTIL THEN we would stay in America just a little bit longer and work for them, for without us, what would they do? Who would pick the strawberries from their fields? Who would get the fruit down from their trees? Who would wash their carrots? Who would scrub their toilets? Who would mend their garments? Who would iron their shirts? Who would fluff their pillows? Who would change their sheets? Who would cook their breakfasts? Who would clear their tables? Who would soothe their children? Who would bathe their elderly? Who would listen to their stories? Who would keep their secrets? Who would tell their lies? Who would flatter them? Who would sing for them? Who would dance for them? Who would weep for them? Who would turn the other cheek for them and then one day—because we were tired, because we were old, because we could—forgive them? *Only a fool.* And so we folded up our kimonos and put them away in our trunks and did not take them out again for years.

BABIES

We gave birth under oak trees, in summer, in 113-degree heat. We gave birth beside woodstoves in one-room shacks on the coldest nights of the year. We gave birth on windy islands in the Delta, six months after we arrived, and the babies were tiny, and translucent, and after three days they died. We gave birth nine months after we arrived to perfect babies with full heads of black hair. We gave birth in dusty vineyard camps in Elk Grove and Florin. We gave birth on remote farms in the Imperial Valley with the help of only our husbands, who had learned from *The Housewife's Companion* what to do. *First you bring the pan water to a boil* ... We gave birth in Rialto by the light of a kerosene lantern on top of an old silk quilt we had brought over with us in our trunk from Japan. *It still had my mother's smell.* We gave birth like Makiyo, in a barn out in Maxwell, while lying on a thick bed of straw. *I wanted to be near the animals.* We gave birth alone, in an apple orchard in Sebastopol, after searching for firewood one unusually warm autumn morning high up in the hills. *I cut her navel string with my knife and carried her home in my arms.* We gave birth in a tent in Livingston with the help of a Japanese midwife who had traveled twenty miles on horseback to see us from the next town. We gave birth in towns where no doctor would see us, and we washed out the afterbirth ourselves. *I watched my mother do it many times.* We gave birth in towns with only one doctor, whose prices we could not afford. We gave birth with the assistance of Dr. Ringwalt, who refused to let us pay him his fee. "You keep it," he said. We gave birth among our own, at the Takahashi Clinic of Midwifery on Clement Street in San Francisco. We gave birth at the Kuwabara Hospital on North Fifth Street in San Jose. We gave birth on a bumpy country road in Castroville in the back of our husband's Dodge truck. *The baby came too fast.* We gave birth on a dirt floor covered with newspapers in a bunkhouse in French Camp to the biggest baby the midwife had ever seen in her life. *Twelve and a half pounds.* We gave birth with the help of the fish seller's wife, Mrs. Kondo, who had known our mother back home in Japan. *She was the second prettiest girl in the village.* We gave birth behind a lace curtain at Adachi's Barbershop in Gardena while our husband was giving Mr. Ota his weekly shave. We gave birth quickly, after hours, in the apartment above Higo Ten Cent. We gave birth while gripping the bedpost and cursing our husband—*You did this!*—and he swore he would never touch us again. We gave birth at five in the morning in the pressing room at the Eagle Hand Laundry and that night our husband began kissing us in bed. *I said to him, "Can't you wait?"* We gave birth quietly, like our mothers, who never cried out or complained. *She worked in the rice paddies until the day she felt her first pangs.* We gave birth weeping, like Nogiku, who came down with fever and could not get out of bed for three months. We gave birth easily, in two hours, and then got a headache that stayed with us for five years. We gave birth six weeks after our husband had left us to a child we now wish we had never given away. *After her I was never able to conceive another.* We gave birth secretly, in the woods, to a child our husband knew was not his. We gave birth on top of a faded floral bedspread in a brothel in Oakland while listening to the grunts coming through the wall from the next room. We gave birth in a boardinghouse in Petaluma, two weeks after moving out of Judge Carmichael's place up on Russian Hill. We gave birth after saying good-bye to our mistress, Mrs. Lippincott, who did not want a pregnant maid greeting guests at her door. *It just wouldn't look right.* We gave birth with the help of the foreman's wife, Señora Santos, who grabbed our thighs and told us to push. *Empuje! Empuje! Empuje!* We gave birth while our husband was out gambling in Chinatown and when he came home drunk the next morning we did not speak to him for five days. *He lost our entire season's earnings in one night.* We gave birth during the Year of the Monkey. We gave birth during the Year of the Rooster. We gave birth during the Year of the Dog and the Dragon and the Rat. We gave birth, like Urako, on the day of the full moon. We gave birth on a Sunday, in a shed in Encinitas, and the next day we tied the baby onto our back and went out to pick berries in the fields. We gave birth to so many children we quickly lost track of the years. We gave birth to Nobuo and Shojiro and Ayako. We gave birth to Tameji, who looked just like our brother, and stared into his face with joy. *Oh, it's you!* We gave birth to Eikichi, who looked just like our neighbor, and after that our husband would not look us in the eye. We gave birth to Misuzu, who came out with her umbilical cord wrapped around her neck like a rosary, and we knew she would one day be a priestess. *It's a sign from the Buddha.* We gave birth to Daisuke, who had long earlobes, and we knew he would one day be rich. We gave birth to Masaji, who came to us late, in our forty-fifth year, just when we had given up all hope of ever producing an heir. *I thought I'd dropped my last egg long ago.* We gave birth to Fujiko, who instantly seemed to recognize the sound of her father's voice. *He used to sing to her every night in the womb.* We gave birth to Yukiko, whose name means "snow." We gave birth to Asano, who had thick thighs and a short neck and would have made a much better boy. We gave birth to Kamechiyo, who was so ugly we feared we would never be able to find her a mate. *She had a face that could stop an earthquake.* We gave birth to babies that were so beautiful we could not believe they were ours. We gave birth to babies that were American citizens and in whose names we could finally lease land. We gave birth to babies with colic. We gave birth to babies with clubfeet. We gave birth to babies that were sickly and blue. We gave birth without our mothers, who would have known exactly what to do. We gave birth to babies with six fingers and looked the other way as the midwife began to sharpen her knife. *You must have eaten a crab during your pregnancy.* We contracted gonorrhea on our first night with our husband

and gave birth to babies that were blind. We gave birth to twins, which were considered bad luck, and asked the midwife to make one a "day visitor." *You decide which one.* We gave birth to eleven children in fifteen years but only seven would survive. We gave birth to six boys and three girls before we were thirty and then one night we pushed our husband off of us and said, quietly, "That's enough." Nine months later we gave birth to Sueko, whose name means "last." "Oh, another one!" our husband said. We gave birth to five girls and five boys at regular eighteen-month intervals and then one day five years later we gave birth to Toichi, whose name means "eleven." *He's the caboose.* We gave birth even though we had poured cold water over our stomachs and jumped off the porch many times. *I couldn't shake it loose.* We gave birth even though we had drunk the medicine the midwife had given us to prevent us from giving birth one more time. *My husband was ill with pneumonia and my work was needed outside in the fields.* We did not give birth for the first four years of our marriage and then we made an offering to Inari and gave birth to six boys in a row. We gave birth to so many babies that our uterus slipped out and we had to wear a special girdle to keep it inside. We almost gave birth but the baby was turned sideways and all that came out was an arm. We almost gave birth but the baby's head was too big and after three days of pushing we looked up at our husband and said, "Please forgive me," and died. We gave birth but the baby was too weak to cry so we left her out, overnight, in a crib by the stove. *If she makes it through till morning then she's strong enough to live.* We gave birth but the baby was both girl and boy and we smothered it quickly with rags. We gave birth but our milk never came in and after one week the baby was dead. We gave birth but the baby had already died in the womb and we buried her, naked, in the fields, beside a stream, but have moved so many times since we can no longer remember where she is.

THE CHILDREN

We laid them down gently, in ditches and furrows and wicker baskets beneath the trees. We left them lying naked, atop blankets, on woven straw mats at the edges of the fields. We placed them in wooden apple boxes and nursed them every time we finished hoeing a row of beans. When they were older, and more rambunctious, we sometimes tied them to chairs. We strapped them onto our backs in the dead of winter in Redding and went out to prune the grapevines but some mornings it was so cold that their ears froze and bled. In early summer, in Stockton, we left them in nearby gullies while we dug up and sacked onions and began picking the first plums. We gave them sticks to play with in our absence and called out to them from time to time to let them know we were still there. *Don't bother the dogs. Don't touch the bees. Don't wander away or Papa will get mad.* But when they tired and began to cry out for us we kept on working because if we didn't we knew we would never pay off the debt on our lease. *Mama can't come.* And after a while their voices grew fainter and their crying came to a stop. And at the end of the day when there was no more light in the sky we woke them up from wherever it was they lay sleeping and brushed the dirt from their hair. *It's time to go home.*

SOME OF THEM were stubborn and willful and would not listen to a word we said. Others were more serene than the Buddha. *He came into the world smiling.* One loved her father more than anyone else. One hated bright colors. One would not go anywhere without his tin pail. One weaned herself at the age of thirteen months by pointing to a glass of milk on the counter and telling us, "I want." Several were wise beyond their years. *The fortune-teller told us he was born with the soul of an old man.* They ate at the table like grown-ups. They never cried. They never complained. They never left their chopsticks standing upright in their rice. They played by themselves all day long without making a sound while we worked nearby in the fields. They drew pictures in the dirt for hours. And whenever we tried to pick them up and carry them home they shook their heads and said, "I'm too heavy" or "Mama, rest." They worried about us when we were tired. They worried about us when we were sad. They knew, without our telling them, when our knees were bothering us or it was our time of the month. They slept with us, at night, like puppies, on wooden boards covered with hay, and for the first time since coming to America we did not mind having someone else beside us in the bed.

ALWAYS, we had favorites. Perhaps it was our firstborn, Ichiro, who made us feel so much less lonely than we had been before. *My husband has not spoken to me in more than two years.* Or our second son, Yoichi, who taught himself how to read English by the time he was four. *He's a genius.* Or Sunoko, who always tugged at our sleeve with such fierce urgency and then forgot what it was she wanted to say. "It will come to you later," we would tell her, even though it never did. Some of us preferred our daughters, who were gentle and good, and some of us, like our mothers before us, preferred our sons. *They're the better gain on the farm.* We fed them more than we did their sisters. We sided with them in arguments. We dressed them in nicer clothes. We scraped up our last pennies to take them to the doctor whenever they came down with fever, while our daughters we cared for at home. *I applied a mustard plaster to her chest and said a prayer to the god of wind and bad colds.* Because we knew that our daughters would leave us the moment they married, but our sons would provide for us in our old age.

USUALLY, our husbands had nothing to do with them. They never changed a single diaper. They never washed a dirty dish. They never touched a broom. In the evening, no matter how tired we were when we came in from the fields, they sat down and read the paper while we cooked dinner for the children and stayed up washing and mending piles of clothes until late. They never let us go to sleep before them. They never let us rise after the sun. *You'll set a bad example for the children.* They never gave us even five minutes of rest. They were silent, weathered men who tramped in and out of the house in their muddy overalls muttering to themselves about sucker growth, the price of green beans, how many crates of celery they thought we could pull this year from the fields. They rarely spoke to their children, or even seemed to remember their names. *Tell number three boy not to slouch when he walks.* And if things grew too noisy at the table, they clapped their hands and shouted out, "That's enough!" Their children, in turn, preferred not to speak to their fathers at all. Whenever one of them had something to say it always went through us. *Tell Papa I need a nickel. Tell Papa there's something wrong with one of the horses. Tell Papa he missed a spot shaving. Ask Papa how come he's so old.*

AS SOON AS WE COULD we put them to work in the fields. They picked strawberries with us in San Martin. They picked peas with us in Los Osos. They crawled behind us through the vineyards of Hughson and Del Rey as we cut down the raisin grapes and laid them out to dry on wooden trays in the sun. They hauled water. They cleared brush. They shoveled weeds. They chopped wood. They hoed in the blazing summer heat of the Imperial Valley before their bones were fully formed. Some of them were slow-moving and dreamy and planted entire rows of cauliflower sprouts upside down by mistake. Others could sort tomatoes faster than the fastest of the hired help. Many complained. They had stomachaches. Headaches. Their eyes were itching like crazy from the dust. Some of them pulled on their boots every morning without having to be told. One of them had a favorite pair of clippers, which he sharpened every evening in the barn after supper and would not let anyone else touch. One could not stop thinking about bugs. *They're everywhere.* One sat down one day in the middle of an onion patch and said she wished she'd never been born. And we wondered if we had done the right thing, bringing them into this world. *Not once did we ever have the money to buy them a single toy.*

AND YET they played for hours like calves in the fields. They made swords out of broken grape stakes and dueled to a draw beneath the trees. They made kites out of newspaper and balsa wood and tied knives to the strings and had dogfights on windy days in the sky. They made twist-up dolls out of wire and straw and did evil things to them with sharpened chopsticks in the woods. They played shadow catch shadow on moonlit nights in the orchards, just as we had back home in Japan. They played kick the can and mumblety-peg and jan ken po. They had contests to see who could nail together the most packing crates the night before we went to market and who could hang the longest from the walnut tree without letting go. They folded squares of paper into airplanes and birds and watched them fly away. They collected crows' nests and snake skins, beetle shells, acorns, rusty iron stakes from down by the tracks. They learned the names of the planets. They read each other's palms. *Your life line is unusually short.* They told each other's fortunes. *One day you will take a long journey on a train.* They went out into the barn after supper with their kerosene lanterns and played mama and papa in the loft. *Now slap your belly and make a sound like you're dying.* And on hot summer nights, when it was ninety-eight degrees, they spread their blankets out beneath the peach trees and dreamed of picnics down by the river, a new eraser, a book, a ball, a china doll with blinking violet eyes, leaving home, one day, for the great world beyond.

BEYOND THE FARM, they'd heard, there were strange pale children who grew up entirely indoors and knew nothing of the fields and streams. Some of these children, they'd heard, had never even seen a tree. *Their mothers won't let them go outside and play in the sun.* Beyond the farm, they'd heard, there were fancy white houses with gold-framed mirrors and crystal doorknobs and porcelain toilets that flushed with the yank of a chain. *And they don't even make a smell.* Beyond the farm, they'd heard, there were mattresses stuffed with hard metal springs that were somehow as soft as a cloud (Goro's sister had gone away to work as a maid in the city and when she came back she said that the beds there were so soft she had to sleep on the floor). Beyond the farm, they'd heard, there were mothers who ate their breakfast every morning in bed and fathers who sat on cushioned chairs all day long in their offices shouting orders into a phone—and for this, they got paid. Beyond the farm, they'd heard, wherever you went you were always a stranger and if you got on the wrong bus by mistake you might never find your way home.

THEY CAUGHT TADPOLES and dragonflies down by the creek and put them into glass jars. They watched us kill the chickens. They found the places in the hills where the deer had last slept and lay down in their round nests in the tall, flattened grass. They pulled the tails off of lizards to see how long it would take them to grow back. *Nothing's happening.* They brought home baby sparrows that had fallen from the trees and fed them sweetened rice gruel with a toothpick but in the morning, when they woke, the sparrows were dead. "Nature doesn't care," we told them. They sat on the fence and watched the farmer in the next field over leading his cow up to meet with the bull. They saw a mother cat eating her own kittens. "It happens," we explained. They heard us being taken late at night by our husbands, who would not leave us alone even though we had long ago lost our looks. "It doesn't matter what you look like in the dark," we were told. They bathed with us every evening, out of doors, in giant wooden tubs heated over a fire and sank down to their chins in the hot steaming water. They leaned back their heads. They closed their eyes. They reached out for our hands. They asked us questions. *How do you know when you're dead? What if there were no birds? What if you have red spots all over your body but nothing hurts? Is it true that the Chinese really eat pigs' feet?*

THEY HAD THINGS to keep them safe. A red bottle cap. A glass marble. A postcard of two Russian beauties strolling along the Songhua River sent to them by an uncle who was stationed in Manchuria. They had lucky white feathers that they carried with them at all times in their pockets, and stones wrapped in soft cloth that they pulled out of drawers and held—just for a moment, until the bad feeling went away—in their hands. They had secret words that they whispered to themselves whenever they felt afraid. They had favorite trees that they climbed up into whenever they wanted to be alone. *Everyone please go away.* They had favorite sisters in whose arms they could instantly fall asleep. They had hated older brothers with whom they refused to be left alone in a room. *He'll kill me.* They had dogs from whom they were inseparable and to whom they could tell all the things they could not tell anyone else. *I broke Papa's pipe and buried it under a tree.* They had their own rules. *Never sleep with your pillow facing toward the north* (Hoshiko had gone to sleep with her pillow facing toward the north and in the middle of the night she stopped breathing and died). They had their own rituals. *You must always throw salt where a hobo has been.* They had their own beliefs. *If you see a spider in the morning you will have good luck. If you lie down after eating you will turn into a cow. If you wear a basket on your head you will stop growing. A single flower means death.*

WE TOLD THEM stories about tongue-cut sparrows and grateful cranes and baby doves that always remembered to let their parents perch on the higher branch. We tried to teach them manners. *Never point with your chopsticks. Never suck on your chopsticks. Never take the last piece of food from a plate.* We praised them when they were kind to others but told them not to expect to be rewarded for their good deeds. We scolded them whenever they tried to talk back.

We taught them never to accept a handout. We taught them never to brag. We taught them everything we knew. A fortune begins with a penny. It is better to suffer ill than to do ill. You must give back whatever you receive. Don't be loud like the Americans. Stay away from the Chinese. *They don't like us.* Watch out for the Koreans. *They hate us.* Be careful around the Filipinos. *They're worse than the Koreans.* Never marry an Okinawan. *They're not real Japanese.*

IN THE COUNTRYSIDE, especially, we often lost them early. To diphtheria and the measles. Tonsillitis. Whooping cough. Mysterious infections that turned gangrenous overnight. One of them was bitten by a poisonous black spider in the outhouse and came down with fever. One was kicked in the stomach by our favorite gray mule. One disappeared while we were sorting the peaches in the packing shed and even though we looked under every rock and tree for her we never did find her and after that we were never the same. *I lost the will to live.* One tumbled out of the truck while we were driving the rhubarb to market and fell into a coma from which he never awoke. One was kidnapped by a pear picker from a nearby orchard whose advances we had repeatedly rebuffed. *I should have just told him yes.* Another was badly burned when the moonshine still exploded out back behind the barn and lived for only a day. *The last thing she said to me was "Mama, don't forget to look up at the sky."* Several drowned. One in the Calaveras River. One in the Nacimiento. One in an irrigation ditch. One in a laundry tub we knew we should not have left out overnight. And every year, in August, on the Feast of the Dead, we lit white paper lanterns on their gravestones and welcomed their spirits back to earth for a day. And at the end of that day, when it was time for them to leave, we set the paper lanterns afloat on the river to guide them safely home. For they were Buddhas now, who resided in the Land of Bliss.

A FEW OF US were unable to have them, and this was the worst fate of all. For without an heir to carry on the family name the spirits of our ancestors would cease to exist. *I feel like I came all the way to America for nothing.* Sometimes we tried going to the faith healer, who told us that our uterus was the wrong shape and there was nothing that could be done. "Your destiny has been settled by the gods," she said to us, and then she showed us to the door. Or we consulted the acupuncturist, Dr. Ishida, who took one look at us and said, "Too much yang," and gave us herbs to nourish our yin and blood. And three months later we found ourselves miscarrying yet again. Sometimes we were sent by our husband back home to Japan, where the rumors would follow us for the rest of our lives. "Divorced," the neigh-bors would whisper. And, "I hear she's dry as a gourd." Sometimes we tried cutting off all our hair and offering it to the goddess of fertility if only she would make us con-ceive, but still, every month, we continued to bleed. And even though our husband had told us it made no difference to him whether he became a father or not—the only thing he wanted, he had said to us, was to grow old by our side—we could not stop thinking of the children we'd never had. *Every night I can hear them playing outside my window in the trees.*

IN J-TOWN they lived with us eight and nine to a room behind our barbershops and bathhouses and in tiny unpainted apartments that were so dark we had to leave the lights on all day long. They chopped carrots for us in our restaurants. They stacked apples for us at our fruit stands. They climbed up onto their bicycles and delivered bags of groceries to our customers' back doors. They separated the colors from the whites in our basement laundries and quickly learned to tell the difference between a red wine stain and blood. They swept the floors of our boardinghouses. They changed towels. They stripped sheets. They made up the beds. They opened doors on things that should never be seen. *I thought he was praying but he was dead.* They brought supper every evening to the elderly widow in 4A from Nagasaki, Mrs. Kawamura, who worked as a chambermaid at the Hotel Drexel and had no children of her own. *My husband was a gambler who left me with only forty-five cents.* They played go in the lobby with the bachelor, Mr. Morita, who started out as a presser at the Empress Hand Laundry thirty years ago and still worked there as a presser to this day. *It all went by so fast.* They trailed their fathers from one yard to the next as they made their gardening rounds and learned how to trim the hedges and mow the grass. They waited for us on wooden slatted benches in the park while we finished cleaning the houses across the street. *Don't talk to strangers,* we told them. *Study hard. Be patient. Whatever you do, don't end up like me.*

AT SCHOOL they sat in the back of the classroom in their homemade clothes with the Mexicans and spoke in timid, faltering voices. They never raised their hands. They never smiled. At recess they huddled together in a corner of the school yard and whispered among themselves in their secret, shameful language. In the cafeteria they were always last in line for lunch. Some of them—our firstborns—hardly knew any English and whenever they were called upon to speak their knees began to shake. One of them, when asked her name by the teacher, replied, "Six," and the laughter rang in her ears for days. Another said his name was Table, and for the rest of his life that was what he was called. Many of them begged us not to be sent back, but within weeks, it seemed, they could name all the animals in English and read aloud every sign that they saw whenever we went shopping downtown—the street of the tall timber poles, they told us, was called State Street, and the street of the unfriendly barbers was Grove, and the bridge from which Mr. Itami had jumped after the stock market collapsed was the Last Chance Bridge—and wherever they went they were able to make their desires known. *One chocolate malt, please.*

ONE BY ONE all the old words we had taught them began to disappear from their heads. They forgot the names of the flowers in Japanese. They forgot the names of the colors. They forgot the names of the fox god and the thunder god and the god of poverty, whom we could never escape. *No matter how long we live in this country they'll never let us buy land.* They forgot the name of the water goddess, Mizu Gami, who protected our rivers and streams and insisted that we keep our wells clean. They forgot the words for snow-light and bell cricket and fleeing in the night. They forgot what to say at the altar to our dead ancestors, who watched over us night and day. They forgot how to count. They forgot how to pray. They spent their days now living in the new language, whose twenty-six letters still eluded us even though we had been in America for years. *All I learned was the letter x so I could sign my name at the bank.* They pronounced their *l*'s and *r*'s with ease. And even when we sent them to the Buddhist church on Saturdays to study Japanese they did not learn a thing. *The only reason my children go is to get out of working in the store.* But whenever we heard them talking out loud in their sleep the words that came out of their mouths came out—we were sure of it—in Japanese.

THEY GAVE THEMSELVES new names we had not chosen for them and could barely pronounce. One called herself Doris. One called herself Peggy. Many called themselves George. Saburo was called Chinky by all the others because he looked just like a Chinaman. Toshitachi was called Harlem because his skin was so dark. Etsuko was given the name Esther by her teacher, Mr. Slater, on her first day of school. "It's his mother's name," she explained. To which we replied, "So is yours." Sumire called herself Violet. Shizuko was Sugar. Makoto was just Mac. Shigeharu Takagi joined the Baptist church at the age of nine and changed his name to Paul. Edison Kobayashi was born lazy but had a photographic memory and could tell you the name of every person he'd ever met. Grace Sugita didn't like ice cream. *Too cold.* Kitty Matsutaro expected nothing and got nothing in return. Six-foot-four Tiny Honda was the biggest Japanese we'd ever seen. Mop Yamasaki had long hair and liked to dress like a girl. Lefty Hayashi was the star pitcher at Emerson Junior High. Sam Nishimura had been sent to Tokyo to receive a proper Japanese education and had just returned to America after six and a half years. *They made him start all over again in the first grade.* Daisy Takada had perfect posture and liked to do things in sets of four. Mabel Ota's father had gone bankrupt three times. Lester Nakano's family bought all their clothes at the Goodwill. Tommy Takayama's mother was—everyone knew it—a whore. *She has six different children by five different men. And two of them are twins.*

SOON we could barely recognize them. They were taller than we were, and heavier. They were loud beyond belief. *I feel like a duck that's hatched goose's eggs.* They preferred their own company to ours and pretended not to understand a word that we said. Our daughters took big long steps, in the American manner, and moved with undignified haste. They wore their garments too loose. They swayed their hips like mares. They chattered away like coolies the moment they came home from school and said whatever popped into their minds. *Mr. Dempsey has a folded ear.* Our sons grew enormous. They insisted on eating bacon and eggs every morning for breakfast instead of bean-paste soup. They refused to use chopsticks. They drank gallons of milk. They poured ketchup all over their rice. They spoke perfect English just like on the radio and whenever they caught us bowing before the kitchen god in the kitchen and clapping our hands they rolled their eyes and said, "Mama, *please.*"

MOSTLY, they were ashamed of us. Our floppy straw hats and threadbare clothes. Our heavy accents. *Every sing oh righ?* Our cracked, callused palms. Our deeply lined faces black from years of picking peaches and staking grape plants in the sun. They longed for real fathers with briefcases who went to work in a suit and tie and only mowed the grass on Sundays. They wanted different and better mothers who did not look so worn out. *Can't you put on a little lipstick?* They dreaded rainy days in the country when we came to pick them up after school in our battered old farm trucks. They never invited over friends to our crowded homes in J-town. *We live like beggars.* They would not be seen with us at the temple on the Emperor's birthday. They would not celebrate the annual Freeing of the Insects with us at the end of summer in the park. They refused to join hands and dance with us in the streets on the Festival of the Autumnal Equinox. They laughed at us whenever we insisted that they bow to us first thing in the morning and with each passing day they seemed to slip further and further from our grasp.

SOME OF THEM developed unusually good vocabularies and became the best students in their class. They won prizes for best essay on California wildflowers. They received highest honors in science. They had more gold stars than anyone else on the teacher's chart. Others fell behind every year during harvest season and had to repeat the same grade twice. One got pregnant at fourteen and was sent away to live with her grandparents on a silkworm farm in remote western Japan. *Every week she writes to me asking when she can come home.* One took his own life. Several quit school. A few ran wild. They formed their own gangs. They made up their own rules. *No knives. No girls. No Chinese allowed.* They went around late at night looking for other people to fight. *Let's go beat up some Filipinos.* And when they were too lazy to leave the neighborhood they stayed at home and fought among themselves. *You goddamn Jap!* Others kept their heads down and tried not to be seen. They went to no parties (they were invited to no parties). They played no instruments (they had no instruments to play). They never got Valentines (they never sent Valentines). They didn't like to dance (they didn't have the right shoes). They floated ghostlike, through the halls, with their eyes turned away and their books clutched to their chests, as though lost in a dream. If someone called them a name behind their back they did not hear it. If someone called them a name to their face they just nodded and walked on. If they were given the oldest textbooks to use in math class they shrugged and took it in stride. *I never really liked algebra anyway.* If their pictures appeared at the end of the yearbook they pretended not to mind. "That's just the way it is," they said to themselves. And, "So what?" And, "Who cares?" Because they knew that no matter what they did they would never really fit in. *We're just a bunch of Buddhaheads.*

THEY LEARNED which mothers would let them come over (Mrs. Henke, Mrs. Woodruff, Mrs. Alfred Chandler III) and which would not (all the other mothers). They learned which barbers would cut their hair (the Negro barbers) and which barbers to avoid (the grumpy barbers on the south side of Grove). They learned that there were certain things that would never be theirs: higher noses, fairer complexions, longer legs that might be noticed from afar. *Every morning I do my stretching exercises but it doesn't seem to help.* They learned when they could go swimming at the YMCA—*Colored days are on Mondays*—and when they could go to the picture show at the Pantages Theater downtown (never). They learned that they should always call the restaurant first. *Do you serve Japanese?* They learned not to go out alone during the daytime and what to do if they found themselves cornered in an alley after dark. *Just tell them you know judo.* And if that didn't work, they learned to fight back with their fists. *They respect you when you're strong.* They learned to find protectors. They learned to hide their anger. *No, of course. I don't mind. That's fine. Go ahead.* They learned never to show their fear. They learned that some people are born luckier than others and that things in this world do not always go as you plan.

STILL, they dreamed. One swore she would one day marry a preacher so she wouldn't have to pick berries on Sundays. One wanted to save up enough money to buy his own farm. One wanted to become a tomato grower like his father. One wanted to become anything but. One wanted to plant a vineyard. One wanted to start his own label. *I'd call it Fukuda Orchards.* One could not wait until the day she got off the ranch. One wanted to go to college even though no one she knew had ever left the town. *I know it's crazy, but . . .* One loved living out in the country and never wanted to leave. *It's better here. Nobody knows who we are.* One wanted something more but could not say exactly what it was. *This just isn't enough.* One wanted a Swing King drum set with hi-hat cymbals. One wanted a spotted pony. One wanted his own paper route. One wanted her own room, with a lock on the door. *Anyone who came in would have to knock first.* One wanted to become an artist and live in a garret in Paris. One wanted to go to refrigeration school. *You can do it through the mail.* One wanted to build bridges. One wanted to play the piano. One wanted to operate his own fruit stand alongside the highway instead of working for somebody else. One wanted to learn shorthand at the Merritt Secretarial Academy and get an inside job in an office. *Then I'd have it made.* One wanted to become the next Great Togo on the professional wrestling circuit. One wanted to become a state senator. One wanted to cut hair and open her own salon. One had polio and just wanted to breathe without her iron lung. One wanted to become a master seamstress. One wanted to become a teacher. One wanted to become a doctor. One wanted to become his sister. One wanted to become a gangster. One wanted to become a star. And even though we saw the darkness coming we said nothing and let them dream on.

TRAITORS

The rumors began to reach us on the second day of the war.

THERE WAS TALK of a list. Some people being taken away in the middle of the night. A banker who went to work and never came home. A barber who disappeared during his lunch break. A few fishermen who had gone missing. Here and there, a boardinghouse, raided. A business, seized. A newspaper shut down. But this was all happening somewhere else. In distant valleys and faraway towns. In the big city, where all the women wore high heels and lipstick and danced until late in the night. "Nothing to do with us," we said. We were simple women who lived quietly and kept to ourselves. Our own husbands would be safe.

FOR SEVERAL DAYS we stayed inside with our shades drawn and listened to the news of the war on the radio. We removed our names from our mailboxes. We brought in our shoes from the front porch. We did not send our children to school. At night we bolted our doors and spoke among ourselves in whispers. We closed our windows tight. Our husbands drank more than usual and stumbled early into bed. Our dogs fell asleep at our feet. No men came to our doors.

CAUTIOUSLY, we began to emerge from our homes. It was December and our older daughters had already left to work as maids in distant towns and the days were quiet and still. The darkness fell early. We rose every morning before dawn in the countryside and went out into the vineyards and pruned back the grapevines. We pulled up carrots from the cold, damp earth. We cut celery. We bunched broccoli. We dug deep furrows into the soil to catch the rain when it fell. Hawks drifted down through the rows of trees in the almond orchards and at dusk we could hear the coyotes calling out to one another in the hills. In J-town we gathered every evening in each other's kitchens and exchanged the latest news. Perhaps there had been a raid in the next county over. A town surrounded after dark. A dozen houses searched. Telephone wires had been cut. Desks overturned. Documents confiscated. A few more men crossed off the list. "Grab your toothbrush," they were told, and that was it, they were never heard from again.

SOME SAID that the men had been put on trains and sent far away, over the mountains, to the coldest part of the country. Some said they were enemy collaborators and would be deported within days. Some said they had been shot. Many of us dismissed the rumors as rumors but found ourselves spreading them—wildly, recklessly, and seemingly against our own will—nonetheless. Others of us refused to speak of the missing men by day but at night they came to us in our dreams. A few of us dreamed we were the missing men ourselves. One of us—Chizuko, who ran the kitchen at the Kearney Ranch and always liked to be prepared—packed a small suitcase for her husband and left it beside their front door. Inside was a toothbrush, a shaving kit, a bar of soap, a bar of chocolate—*his favorite*—and a clean change of clothes. These were the things she knew he would need to bring with him if his name came up next on the list. Always, though, there was the vague but nagging fear that she had left something out, some small but crucial item that, on some unknown date in some unknown court in the future, would serve as incontestable proof of her husband's innocence. Only what, she asked herself, could that small item be? A Bible? A pair of reading glasses? A different kind of soap? Something more fragrant, perhaps? Something more manly? *I hear they arrested a Shinto priest in the valley for owning a toy bamboo flute.*

WHAT DID WE KNOW, exactly, about the list? The list had been drawn up hastily, on the morning of the attack. The list had been drawn up more than one year ago. The list had been in existence for almost ten years. The list was divided into three categories: "known dangerous" (Category A), "potentially dangerous" (Category B), and "pro-Axis inclinations" (Category C). It was nearly impossible to get your name on the list. It was extremely easy to get your name on the list. Only people who belonged to our race were on the list. There were Germans and Italians on the list, but their names appeared toward the bottom. The list was written in indelible red ink. The list was typewritten on index cards. The list did not exist. The list existed, but only in the mind of the director of military intelligence, who was known for his perfect recall. The list was a figment of our imaginations. The list contained over five hundred names. The list contained over five thousand names. The list was endless. Every time an arrest was made another name was crossed off the list. Every time a name was crossed off the list a new name was added to it. New names were added to the list daily. Weekly. Hourly.

A FEW OF US began receiving anonymous letters in the mail, informing us that our own husbands would be next. *I'd think about getting out of town if I were you.* Others reported that their husbands had been threatened by angry Filipino workers in the fields. *They came at him with their vegetable knives.* Hitomi, who had worked as a housekeeper at the Prince estate for more than ten years, was held up at gunpoint in broad daylight as she was heading back into town. Mitsuko went out one evening before supper to gather the eggs from her chickens and saw her laundry on fire on the line. And we knew this was only the beginning.

OVERNIGHT, our neighbors began to look at us differently. Maybe it was the little girl down the road who no longer waved to us from her farmhouse window. Or the longtime customers who suddenly disappeared from our restaurants and stores. Or our mistress, Mrs. Trimble, who pulled us aside one morning as we were mopping her kitchen and whispered into our ear, "Did you know that the war was coming?" Club ladies began boycotting our fruit stands because they were afraid our produce might be tainted with arsenic. Insurance companies canceled our insurance. Banks froze our bank accounts. Milkmen stopped delivering milk to our doors. "Company orders," one tearful milkman explained. Children took one look at us and ran away like frightened deer. Little old ladies clutched their purses and froze up on the sidewalk at the sight of our husbands and shouted out, "They're here!" And even though our husbands had warned us—*They're afraid*—still, we were unprepared. Suddenly, to find ourselves the enemy.

IT WAS ALL, of course, because of the stories in the papers. They said that thousands of our men had sprung into action, with clockwork precision, the moment the attack on the island had begun. They said we had flooded the roads with our run-down trucks and jalopies. They said we had signaled to the enemy planes with flares from our fields. They said that the week before the attack several of our children had bragged to their classmates that "something big" was about to happen. They said that those same children, when questioned further by their teachers, had reported that their parents had celebrated the news of the attack for days. *They were shouting banzais.* They said that in the event of a second attack here on the mainland anyone whose name appeared on the list would more than likely rise up to assist the enemy. They said that our truck farmers were foot soldiers in a vast underground army. *They've got thousands of weapons down below in their vegetable cellars.* They said that our houseboys were intelligence agents in disguise. They said that our gardeners were all hiding shortwave radio transmitters in their garden hoses and when the Pacific zero hour struck we'd get busy at once. Burst dams. Burning oil fields. Bombed bridges. Blasted roads. Blocked tunnels. Poisoned reservoirs. And what was to stop one of us from walking into a crowded marketplace with a stick of dynamite tied to our waist? *Nothing.*

EVERY EVENING, at dusk, we began burning our things: old bank statements and diaries, Buddhist family altars, wooden chopsticks, paper lanterns, photographs of our unsmiling relatives back home in the village in their strange country clothes. *I watched my brother's face turn to ash and float up into the sky.* We set fire to our white silk wedding kimonos out of doors, in our apple orchards, in the furrows between the trees. We poured gasoline over our ceremonial dolls in metal trash cans in J-town back alleys. We got rid of anything that might suggest our husbands had enemy ties. Letters from our sisters. *East Neighbor's son has run away with the umbrella maker's wife.* Letters from our fathers. *The trains have been electrified and now whenever you go through a tunnel you do not get soot all over your face!* Letters from our mothers written to us on the day we'd left home. *I can still see your footprints in the mud down by the river.* And we wondered why we had insisted for so long on clinging to our strange, foreign ways. *We've made them hate us.*

THE NIGHTS GREW LONGER, and colder, and every day we learned of a few more men who had been taken away. A produce distributor in the southland. A judo instructor. A silk importer. A shipping clerk in the city who was returning to his office from a late lunch. *Apprehended at the crosswalk while waiting for the light to turn green.* An onion grower in the Delta who was suspected of plotting to blow up the levee. *They found a box of stumping powder in his barn.* A travel agent. A language instructor. A lettuce farmer on the coast who was accused of using his flashlight to send signals to enemy ships out at sea.

CHIYOMI'S HUSBAND began going to sleep with his clothes on, just in case tonight was the night. Because the most shameful thing, he had told her, would be to be taken away in his pajamas (Eiko's husband had been taken away in his pajamas). Asako's husband had become obsessed with his shoes. *He polishes them every night to a high shine and lines them up at the foot of the bed.* Yuriko's husband, a traveling fertilizer salesman who had been less than faithful to her over the years, could only fall asleep now if she was right there by his side. "It's a little late," she said, "but what can you do? Once you marry, it's for life." Hatsumi's husband whispered a quick prayer to the Buddha every night before climbing into bed. Some nights he even prayed to Jesus, because what if he was the one true god? Masumi's husband suffered from nightmares. It was dark and all the streets had disappeared. The sea was rising. The sky was falling. He was trapped on an island. He was lost in a desert. He had misplaced his wallet and was late to catch a train. He saw his wife standing in a crowd and called out to her but she did not turn around. *All that man has ever given me is grief.*

THE FIRST HEAVY RAINS blew down the last of the leaves from the trees and the days quickly lost their warmth. The shadows slowly lengthened. Our younger children went to school every morning and came home with stories. A girl had swallowed a penny at recess and almost died. Mr. Barnett was trying to grow a mustache again. Mrs. Trachtenberg was in a bad mood. *She's having her monthly.* We spent long days in the orchards with our older sons and husbands, clipping twigs, pruning branches, lopping off the dead limbs that would not bear fruit in the summer or fall. We cooked and cleaned in the suburbs for the families we had been cooking and cleaning for for years. We did the things we had always done, but nothing felt the same. "Every little noise frightens me now," said Onatsu. "A knock on the door. The ringing of a telephone. The barking of a dog. I am constantly listening for footsteps." And whenever a strange car drove through the neighborhood her heart began to pound, for she was sure that her husband's time had come. Sometimes, in her more confused moments, she imagined that it had already happened, and her husband was now gone, and she had to admit, she was almost relieved, for it was the waiting that was most difficult.

FOR THREE DAYS a cold wind blew down from the mountains without stopping. Clouds of dust rose up from the fields and the bare branches of the trees thrashed against an empty gray sky. Gravestones toppled over in our cemeteries. Barn doors flew open. Tin roofs rattled. Favorite dogs ran away. A Chinese laundryman was found unconscious and bleeding on the waterfront and left behind for dead. *They mistook him for one of us.* A barn was set on fire in a remote inland valley and the stench of dead cattle lingered downwind for days.

AT NIGHT we sat in our kitchens with our husbands as they pored over the day's papers, scrutinizing every line, every word, for clues to our fate. We discussed the latest rumors. *I hear they're putting us into work camps to grow food for the troops.* We turned on the radio and listened to the bulletins from the front. The news, of course, was not good. The enemy had sunk six more of our unsinkable battleships. The enemy's planes had been sighted making test runs in our skies. The enemy's submarines were coming closer and closer to our shores. The enemy was planning a combined attack on the coast from without and within and all alert, keen-eyed citizens were being asked to inform the authorities of any fifth columnists who might dwell in our midst. Because anyone, we were reminded, could be a spy. Your butler, your gardener, your florist, your maid.

AT THREE in the morning one of our most prominent berry growers was dragged out of bed and escorted out his front door. He was the first of the men we knew to be taken away. *They're only going after the wealthy farmers,* people said. The following evening a local field hand at the Spiegl Ranch was picked up in his muddy overalls while walking his dog by the reservoir and questioned for three days and three nights in a brightly lit room with no windows before being told he could go home. But when his wife drove down to the station to get him he had no idea who she was. *He thought I was an impostor who was trying to get him to talk.* The next day three women we knew in a nearby town came forward to report that their husbands, too, had been on the list. "They put him in a car," one of them said, "and he was gone." Two days later, one of our competitors—the only other rancher in the valley whose raisin grapes were even half as sweet as ours—was handcuffed to a chair in his kitchen for four hours while three men searched his house and then he was allowed to go free. His wife, people said, had served the men coffee and pie. And we all wanted to know: What kind of pie? Strawberry? Rhubarb? Lemon meringue? And how did the men take their coffee? With sugar or without?

SOME NIGHTS our husbands lay awake for hours going over their pasts again and again, searching for proof that their names, too, might be on the list. Surely there must be something they had said, or done, surely there must be some mistake they had made, surely they must be guilty of *something*, some obscure crime, perhaps, of which they were not even aware. Only what, they asked us, could that obscure crime be? Was it that toast they had given to our homeland at last year's annual summer picnic? Or some remark they may have made about the President's most recent speech? *He called us gangsters.* Or had they made a contribution to the wrong charity—a charity whose secret ties to the enemy they knew nothing about? Could that be it? Or had somebody—somebody, no doubt, with a grudge—filed a false accusation against them with the authorities? One of our customers at the Capitol Laundry, perhaps, to whom we had once been unnecessarily curt? (Was it, then, all *our* fault?) Or a disgruntled neighbor whose flower bed our dog had made use of one too many times? Should they have been friendlier, our husbands asked us. Were their fields too unkempt? Had they kept too much to themselves? Or was their guilt written plainly, and for all the world to see, across their face? Was it their face, in fact, for which they were guilty? Did it fail to please in some way? Worse yet, did it offend?

IN JANUARY we were ordered to register with the authorities and turn over all items of contraband to our local police: guns, bombs, dynamite, cameras, binoculars, knives with blades longer than six inches, signaling devices such as flashlights and flares, anything that might be used to assist the enemy in the event of an attack. Then came the travel restrictions—no people of our ancestry allowed to travel more than five miles from their homes— and the 8:00 p.m. curfew, and even though most of us were not really night people, for the first time in our lives we found ourselves longing to take the occasional midnight stroll. *Just once, with my husband, through the almond groves, to know what it's like.* But at two in the morning when we looked out our windows and saw our friends and neighbors raiding our barns we did not dare set foot out our front doors, for fear that we, too, would be turned in to the police. Because all it took, we knew, was one phone call to get your name on the list. And when our older sons began staying out all night downtown on Saturdays we did not ask them where they had been when they came home late the next morning, or who they had been with, or how much she had cost, or why they were wearing *I Am Chinese* buttons pinned to the collars of their shirts. "Let them have their fun while they can," our husbands said to us. So we wished our sons a civil good morning in the kitchen— *Eggs or coffee?*—and got on with our day.

"WHEN I'M GONE," our husbands said to us. We said to them, "If." They said, "Remember to tip the iceman," and "Always greet the customers by name when they come through the door." They told us where to find the children's birth certificates, and when to ask Pete at the garage to rotate the wheels on the truck. "If you run out of money," they said to us, "sell the tractor." "Sell the greenhouse." "Sell off all the merchandise in the store." They reminded us to watch our posture—*Shoulders back*—and not let the children slip up on their chores. They said, "Stay in touch with Mr. Hauer at the Berry Growers' Association. He is a useful person to know and may be able to help you." They said, "Believe nothing you hear about me." And, "Trust no one." And, "Don't tell the neighbors a thing." They said, "Don't worry about the mice in the ceiling. I'll take care of them when I come home." They reminded us to carry our alien identification cards with us whenever we left the house and avoid all public discussion of the war. If asked, however, to give our opinion, we were to denounce the attack loudly, in a no-nonsense tone of voice. "Do not apologize," they said to us. "Speak only English." "Suppress the urge to bow."

IN THE NEWSPAPERS, and on the radio, we began to hear talk of mass removals. *House to Hold Hearings on National Defense Migration. Governor Urges President to Evacuate All Enemy Aliens from the Coast. Send Them Back to Tojo!* It would happen gradually, we heard, over a period of weeks, if not months. None of us would be forced out overnight. We would be sent far away, to a point of our own choosing deep in the zone of the interior where we could not do anyone any harm. We would be held under protective custody arrest for the duration of the war. Only those of us who lived within one hundred miles of the coast would be removed. Only those of us on the list would be removed. Only those of us who were noncitizens would be removed. Our adult children would be allowed to remain behind to oversee our businesses and farms. Our businesses and farms would be confiscated and put up for auction. *So start liquidating now.* We would be separated from our younger children. We would be sterilized and deported at the earliest practicable date.

WE TRIED to think positive thoughts. If we finished ironing the laundry before midnight our husband's name would be removed from the list. If we bought a ten-dollar war bond our children would be spared. If we sang "The Hemp-Winding Song" all the way through without making a mistake then there would be no list, no laundry, no war bonds, no war. Often, though, at the end of the day, we felt uneasy, as if there was something we had forgotten to do. Had we remembered to close the sluice gate? Turn off the stove? Feed the chickens? Feed the children? Tap the bedpost three times?

IN FEBRUARY the days grew slowly warmer and the first poppies bloomed bright orange in the hills. Our numbers continued to dwindle. Mineko's husband was gone. Takeko's husband was gone. Mitsue's husband was gone. *They found a bullet in the dirt behind his woodshed.* Omiyo's husband was pulled over on the highway for being out on the road five minutes after curfew. Hanayo's husband was arrested at his own dinner table for reasons unknown. "The worst thing he ever did was get a parking ticket," she said. And Shimako's husband, a truck driver for the

Union Fruit Company whom none of us had ever heard utter a word, was apprehended in the dairy aisle of the local grocery for being a spy for the enemy high command. "I knew it all along," someone said. Someone else said, "Next time it could be you."

THE HARDEST THING, Chizuko told us, was not knowing where he was. The first night after her husband's arrest she had woken up in a panic, unable to remember why she was alone. She had reached out and felt the empty bed beside her and thought, *I'm dreaming, this is a nightmare,* but it wasn't, it was real. But she had gotten out of bed anyway and wandered through the house calling out for her husband as she peered into closets and checked under beds. *Just in case.* And when she saw his suitcase still standing there beside the front door she took out the bar of chocolate and slowly began to eat. "He forgot," she said. Yumiko had seen her husband twice in her dreams and he'd told her he was doing all right. It was the dog, she said, that she was most worried about. "She lies around for hours on top of his slippers and growls at me whenever I try to sit on his chair." Fusako confessed that whenever she heard that someone else's husband had been taken away she felt secretly relieved. "You know, 'Better her than me.'" And then, of course, she felt so ashamed. Kanuko admitted that she did not miss her husband at all. "He worked me like a man and kept me pregnant for years." Kyoko said that as far as she knew her husband's name was not on the list. "He's a nurseryman. He loves flowers. There is nothing subversive about him." Nobuko said, "Yes, but you never know." The rest of us held our breath and waited to see what would happen next.

WE FELT CLOSER to our husbands, now, than we ever had before. We gave them the best cuts of meat at supper. We pretended not to notice when they made crumbs. We wiped away their muddy footprints from the floor without comment. At night we did not turn away from them in bed. And if they yelled at us for failing to prepare the bath the way they liked it, or grew impatient and said unkind things—*Twenty years in America and all you can say is "Harro"?*—we held our tongues and tried not to get angry, because what if we woke up the next morning and they were not there? How would we feed the children? How would we pay the rent? *Satoko had to sell off all her furniture.* Who would put out the smudge pots in the middle of the night to protect the fruit trees from an unexpected spring frost? Who would fix the broken tractor hitch? Who would mix the fertilizer? Who would sharpen the plow? Who would calm us down when someone had been rude to us in the market, or called us a less-than-flattering name on the street? Who would grab our arms and shake us when we stomped our feet and told them we'd had it, we were leaving them, we were taking the next boat back home? *The only reason you married me was to get extra help on the farm.*

MORE AND MORE now we began to suspect that there were informers among us. Teruko's husband, people whispered, had turned in a labor foreman at the apple-drying plant with whom she had once had an affair. Fumino's husband had been accused of being pro-Axis by a former business partner who was now desperate for cash. (Informers, we had heard, were paid twenty-five dollars a head.) Kuniko's husband had been denounced as a member of the Black Dragon Society by none other than Kuniko herself. *He was about to leave her for his mistress.* And Ruriko's husband? Korean, his neighbors said. Working undercover. Bankrolled by the government to keep an eye on members of the local Buddhist church. *I saw him taking down license plate numbers in the parking lot.* Several days later he was found badly beaten in a ditch by the side of the road and the next morning he and his family were nowhere to be found. The front door to their house was wide open, their cats had been recently fed, a pot of hot water was still boiling on the stove. And that was that, they were gone. Word of their whereabouts, however, began to reach us within days. *They're down south by the border. They've fled to the next state. They're living in a nice house in the city with a brand-new car and no visible means of support.*

SPRING ARRIVED. The almond trees in the orchards began dropping the last of their petals and the cherry trees were just reaching full bloom. Sun poured down through the branches of the orange trees. Sparrows rustled in the grass. A few more of our men disappeared every day. We tried to keep ourselves busy and be grateful for little things. A friendly nod from a neighbor. A hot bowl of rice.

A bill paid on time. A child safely put to bed. We woke up early every morning and pulled on our field clothes and we plowed and we planted and we hoed. We dug up weeds in our vineyards. We irrigated our squash and peas. Once a week, on Fridays, we put up our hair and went into town to go shopping, but did not stop to say hello to one another when we met on the street. *They'll think we're exchanging secrets.* We rarely visited each other after dark in J-town because of the curfew. We did not linger long after services at church. *Now whenever I speak to someone, I have to ask myself, "Is this someone who will betray me?"* Around our younger children, too, we were careful about what we said. *Chieko's husband was turned in as a spy by his eight-year-old son.* Some of us even began to wonder about our own husbands: *Does he have a secret identity of which I am not aware?*

SOON WE WERE hearing stories of entire communities being taken away. More than ninety percent of our men had been removed from a small town of lettuce growers in a valley to our north. More than one hundred of our men had been removed from the defense zone around the airfield. And down south, in a small fishing town of black shanties on the coast, all people of our descent had been rounded up in a day and a night on a blanket warrant without warning. Their logbooks had been confiscated, their sardine boats placed under guard, their fishing nets cut to shreds and tossed back out into the sea. Because the fishermen, it was said, were not really fishermen, but secret officers of the enemy's imperial navy. *They found their uniforms wrapped up in oil paper at the bottom of their bait boxes.*

SOME OF US went out and began buying sleeping bags and suitcases for our children, just in case we were next. Others of us went about our work as usual and tried to remain calm. *A little more starch on this collar and it'll be fine, now, don't you think?* Whatever would happen would happen, we told ourselves, it was no use tempting the gods. One of us stopped talking. Another of us went out early one morning to water the horses and hung herself in the barn. Fubuki was so anxious that when the evacuation orders were finally posted she let out a sigh of relief, for at last, the waiting had come to an end. Teiko stared at the notice in disbelief and quietly shook her head. "But what about our strawberries?" she asked. "They'll be ready to pick in three weeks." Machiko said she wasn't going, it was as simple as that. "We just renewed our lease for the restaurant." Umeko said we had no choice but to do as we were told. "It's the President's order," she said. And who were we to question the President? "What will the soil be like there?" Takiko's husband wanted to know. How many days of sun would we get? And how many days of rain? Kiko just folded her hands and looked down at her feet. "It's all over," she said softly. At least, Haruyo said, we would all be leaving together. Hisako said, "Yes, but what have we done?" Isino covered her face and wept. "I should have divorced my husband years ago and taken the children back home to my mother in Japan."

FIRST they told us we were being sent to the mountains, so be sure to dress warmly, it would be very very cold. So we went out and bought long woolen underwear and our first warm winter coats. Then we heard we were being sent to the desert, where there were poisonous black snakes and mosquitoes the size of small birds. There were no doctors there, people said, and the place was crawling with thieves. So we went out and bought padlocks and bottles of vitamins for our children, boxes of bandages, sticks of moxa, medicinal plasters, castor oil, iodine, aspirin, gauze. We heard that we could only bring with us one bag apiece so we sewed little cloth knapsacks for our youngest children, with their names embroidered on each. Inside we put pencils and ledgers, toothbrushes, sweaters, brown paper bags filled with rice we had left out to dry on tin trays in the sun. *In case we get separated.* "This is only for a while," we said to them. We told them not to worry. We talked about all the things we would do when we came home. We would eat dinner every night in front of the radio. We would take them to the picture show downtown. We would go to the traveling circus to see the Siamese twins and the lady with the world's smallest head. *No bigger than a plum!*

PALE GREEN BUDS broke on the grapevines in the vineyards and all throughout the valleys the peach trees were flowering beneath clear blue skies. Drifts of wild mustard blossomed bright yellow in the canyons. Larks flew down from the hills. And one by one, in distant cities and towns, our older sons and daughters quit their jobs and dropped out of school and began coming home. They helped us find people to take over our dry cleaners in J-town. They helped us find new tenants for our restaurants. They helped us put up signs in our stores. *Buy Now! Save! Entire Stock Must Be Sold!* They pulled on their overalls in the countryside and helped us prepare for the harvest one last time, for we had been ordered to till our fields until the very end. This was our contribution to the war effort, we were told. An opportunity for us to prove our loyalty. A way to provide fresh fruits and vegetables for the folks on the home front.

JUNKMEN SLOWLY DROVE their trucks down the narrow streets of our neighborhoods, offering us money for our things. Ten dollars for a new stove we had bought for two hundred the year before. Five dollars for a refrigerator. A nickel for a lamp. Neighbors with whom we had never exchanged a word approached us in the fields and asked us if there was anything we wanted to get rid of. That cultivator, perhaps? That harrow? That plow horse? That plow? That Queen Anne rosebush in our front yard they'd been admiring for years? Strangers knocked on our doors. "Got any dogs?" one man asked. His son, he explained, badly wanted a new puppy. Another man said he lived alone in a trailer near the shipping yard and would be happy to take a used cat. "It gets lonely, you know." Sometimes we sold hastily, and for whatever we could get, and other times we gave away favorite vases and teapots and tried not to care too much, because our mothers had always told us: *One must not get too attached to the things of this world.*

AS THE DAY of our departure drew nearer we paid our final bills to our creditors and thanked the loyal customers who had stood by us until the very end. Sheriff Burckhardt's wife, Henrietta, who bought five baskets of strawberries every Friday at our fruit stand and left us a fifty-cent tip. *Please buy yourself something nice.* Retired widower Thomas Duffy, who came to our noodle shop every day at half past noon and ordered a plate of chicken fried rice. Ladies' Auxiliary Club president Rosalind Anders, who refused to take her dry cleaning anyplace else. *The Chinese just don't do it right.* We continued to work our fields as we always had, but nothing felt quite real. We nailed together crates to box up crops we would not be able to harvest. We pinched the shoots off of grapevines that would not ripen until after we had left. We turned over the soil and planted tomato seedlings that would come up in late summer, when we were already gone. The days were long and sunny now. The nights were cool. The reservoirs full. The price of sugar snaps was rising. Asparagus was nearing an all-time high. There were green berries on the strawberry plants and in the orchards the nectarine trees would soon be heavy with fruit. *One more week and we would have made a fortune.* And even though we knew we would soon be leaving we kept on hoping that something would happen, and we would not have to go.

PERHAPS THE CHURCH would intervene on our behalf, or the President's wife. Or maybe there had been a terrible misunderstanding and it was really some other people they had meant to take. "The Germans," someone suggested. "Or the Italians," said someone else. Someone else said, "How about the Chinese?" Others of us remained quiet and prepared to leave as best we could. We sent notes to our children's teachers, apologizing to them in our broken English for our children's sudden and unexpected absence from school. We wrote out instructions for future tenants, explaining to them how to work the sticky flue in the fireplace and what to do about the leak in the roof. *Just use a bucket.* We left lotus blossoms for the Buddha outside our temples. We made last visits to our cemeteries and poured water over the gravestones of those of us whose spirits had already passed out of this world. Yoshiye's young son, Tetsuo, who had been gored by an angry bull. The tea merchant's daughter from Yokohama, whose name we could now barely recall. *Died of the Spanish influenza on her fifth day off the boat.* We walked the rows of our vineyards one last time with our husbands, who could not resist pulling up one last weed. We propped up sagging branches in our almond orchards. We checked for worms in our lettuce fields and scooped up handfuls of freshly turned black earth. We did last loads of wash in our laundries. We shuttered our groceries. We swept our floors. We packed our bags. We gathered up our children and from every town in every valley and every city up and down the coast, we left.

THE LEAVES of the trees continued to turn in the wind. The rivers continued to flow. Insects hummed in the grass as always. Crows cawed. The sky did not fall. No President changed his mind. Mitsuko's favorite black hen clucked once and laid a warm brown egg. A green plum fell early from a tree. Our dogs ran after us with balls in their mouths, eager for one last toss, and for once, we had to turn them away. *Go home.* Neighbors peered out at us through their windows. Cars honked. Strangers stared. A boy on a bicycle waved. A startled cat dove under a bed in one of our houses as looters began to break down the front door. Curtains ripped. Glass shattered. Wedding dishes smashed to the floor. And we knew it would only be a matter of time until all traces of us were gone.

LAST DAY

Some of us left weeping. And some of us left singing. One of us left with her hand held over her mouth and hysterically laughing. A few of us left drunk. Others of us left quietly, with our heads bowed, embarrassed and ashamed. There was an old man from Gilroy who left on a stretcher. There was another old man—Natsuko's husband, a retired barber in Florin—who left on crutches with an American Legion cap pulled down low over his head. "Nobody win war. Everybody lose," he said. Most of us left speaking only English, so as not to anger the crowds that had gathered to watch us go. Many of us had lost everything and left saying nothing at all. All of us left wearing white numbered identification tags tied to our collars and lapels. There was a newborn baby from San Leandro who left sleepily, with her eyes half closed, in a swaying wicker basket. Her mother—Shizuma's eldest daughter, Naomi—left anxiously but stylishly in a gray wool skirt and black alligator pumps. "Do you think they'll have milk there?" she kept asking. There was a boy in short pants from Oxnard who left wondering whether or not they'd have swings. Some of us left wearing our very best clothes. Others of us left wearing the only clothes we had. One woman left in fox furs. *The Lettuce*

King's wife, people whispered. One man left barefoot but freshly shaven, with all of his belongings neatly wrapped up in a square of white cloth: a Buddhist rosary, a clean shirt, a lucky pair of dice, a new pair of socks, to be worn in better times. One man from Santa Barbara left carrying a brown leather suitcase covered with faded stickers that said *Paris* and *London* and *Hotel Metropole, Bayreuth.* His wife left three steps behind him carrying a wooden washboard and a book of etiquette she had checked out from the library by Emily Post. "It's not due until next week," she said. There were families from Oakland who left carrying sturdy canvas seabags they had bought the day before at Montgomery Ward. There were families from Fresno who left carrying bulging cardboard boxes. The Tanakas of Gardena left without paying their rent. The Tanakas of Delano, without paying their taxes. The Kobayashis of Biola left after bleaching the top of their stove and washing the floors of their restaurant with buckets of scalding hot water. The Suzukis of Lompoc left little piles of salt outside their doorway to purify their house. The Nishimotos of San Carlos left out bowls of fresh orchids from their nursery on their kitchen table for whoever was moving in next. The Igarashis of Preston packed up until the last moment and left their place a mess. Most of us left in a hurry. Many of us left in despair. A few of us left in disgust, and had no desire to ever come back. One of us left Robert's Island in the Delta clutching a copy of the Bible and humming *"Sakura, sakura."* One of us came from the big city and left wearing her first pair of pants. *They say it's no place for dresses.* One of us left after having her hair done at the Talk of the Town Beauty Salon for the first time in her life. *It's something I've always wanted to do.* One of us left a rice ranch in Willows carrying a tiny Buddhist shrine in her pocket and telling everyone that things would turn out all right in the end. "The gods will look after us," she said. Her husband left in muddy field clothes with their entire life savings stuffed into the toe of his boot. "Fifty cent," he said with a wink and a smile. Some of us left without our husbands, who had been arrested during the first weeks of the war. Some of us left without our children, whom we had sent away years before. *I asked my parents to take care of my two oldest so I could work full-time on the farm.* One man left East First Street in Los Angeles with a white wooden box filled with his wife's ashes hanging from a silk sash around his neck. *He talks to her all day long.* One man left downtown Hayward with a tin of chocolates given to him by the Chinese couple who had taken over the lease on his store. One man left a grape ranch in Dinuba carrying a grudge against his neighbor, Al Petrosian, who had never paid him what he owed for his plow. *You can never trust the Armenians.* One man left Sacramento shaking and empty-handed and shouting out, "It's all yours." Asayo—our prettiest—left the New Ranch in Redwood carrying the same rattan suitcase she had brought over with her twenty-three years ago on the boat. *It still looks brand-new.* Yasuko left her apartment in Long Beach with a letter from a man who was not her husband neatly folded up inside her compact at the bottom of her purse. Masayo left after saying good-bye to her youngest son, Masamichi, at the hospital in San Bruno, where he would be dead of the mumps by the end of the week. Hanako left fearful and coughing, but all she had was a cold. Matsuko left with a headache. Toshiko left with a fever. Shiki left in a trance. Mitsuyo left nauseous and unexpectedly pregnant for the first time in her life at the age of forty-eight. Nobuye left wondering whether or not she had unplugged her iron, which she had used that morning to touch up the pleats of her blouse. "I've got to go *back*," she said to her husband, who stared straight ahead and did not reply. Tora left with a venereal disease she had contracted on her last night at the Welcome Hotel. Sachiko left practicing her ABCs as though it were just another ordinary day. Futaye, who had the best vocabulary of us all, left speechless. Atsuko left heartbroken after saying farewell to all the trees in her orchard. *I planted them as saplings.* Miyoshi left pining for her big horse, Ryuu. Satsuyo left looking for her neighbors, Bob and Florence Eldridge, who had promised to come say good-bye. Tsugino left with a clear conscience after shouting a long-held and ugly secret down into a well. *I filled the baby's mouth with ashes and it died.* Kiyono left the farm on White Road convinced she was being punished for a sin she had committed in a previous life. *I must have stepped on a spider.* Setsuko left her house in Gridley after killing all the chickens in her backyard. Chiye left Glendale still grieving for her oldest daughter, Misuzu, who had thrown herself in front of a trolley car five years before. Suteko, who had no

children of her own, left feeling as though life had somehow passed her by. Shizue left Camp No. 8 on Webb
Island chanting a sutra that had just come back to her after
thirty-four years. *My father used to recite it every morning at
the altar.* Katsuno left her husband's laundry in San Diego
mumbling, "Somebody wake me up, please." Fumiko left a
boardinghouse in Courtland apologizing for any trouble
she might have caused. Her husband left telling her to pick
up the pace and please keep her mouth shut. Misuyo left
graciously, and with ill will toward none. Chiyoko, who
had always insisted that we call her Charlotte, left insisting
that we call her Chiyoko. *I've changed my mind one last time.*
Iyo left with an alarm clock ringing from somewhere deep
inside her suitcase but did not stop to turn it off. Kimiko
left her purse behind on the kitchen table but would not
remember until it was too late. Haruko left a tiny laughing
brass Buddha up high, in a corner of the attic, where he is
still laughing to this day. Takako left a bag of rice beneath
the floorboards of her kitchen so her family would have
something to eat when they returned. Misayo left out a
pair of wooden sandals on her front porch so it would look
like someone was still home. Roku left her mother's silver mirror with her neighbor, Louise Hastings, who had
promised to keep it for her until she came back. *I will help
you in any way I can.* Matsuyo left wearing a pearl necklace
given to her by her mistress, Mrs. Bunting, whose house in
Wilmington she had kept spotless for twenty-one years.
Half my life. Sumiko left with an envelope filled with cash
given to her by her second husband, Mr. Howell, of Mon-

tecito, who had recently informed her that he would not be accompanying her on the trip. *She gave him back his ring.* Chiyuno left Colma thinking of her younger brother, Jiro, who had been sent to the leper colony on the island of Oshima in the summer of 1909. *We never spoke of him again.* Ayumi left Edenville wondering whether or not she had remembered to pack her lucky red dress. *I don't feel like myself without it.* Nagako left El Cerrito filled with regret for all the things she had not done. *I wanted to visit my home village one last time and burn incense at my father's grave.* Her daughter, Evelyn, left telling her, "Hurry, hurry, Mama, we're late." There was a woman of uncommon beauty whom none of us had ever seen who left blinking and confused. Her husband, people said, had kept her locked up in his basement so no other man could lay eyes on her face. There was a man from San Mateo who left carrying a set of golf clubs and a case of Old Parr Scotch. *I hear he used to be Charlie Chaplin's personal valet.* There was a man of the cloth—Reverend Shibata of the First Baptist Church—who left urging everyone to forgive and forget. There was a man in a shiny brown suit—fry cook Kanda of Yabu Noodle—who left urging Reverend Shibata to give it a rest. There was a national fly-casting champion from Pismo Beach who left carrying his favorite bamboo fishing pole and a book of poems by Robert Frost. *It's all I really need.* There was a group of champion bridge players from Monterey who left grinning and flush with cash. There was a family of sharecroppers from Pajaro who left wondering whether or not they would ever see their valley again. There were aging sunburned bachelors who left from everywhere and nowhere all at once. *They've been following the crops for years.* There was a gardener from Santa Maria who left with a rhododendron cutting from his master's front yard and a pocket filled with seeds. There was a grocer from Oceanside who left with a worthless check written out to him by a truck driver who had offered to buy all the fixtures in his store. There was a pharmacist from Stockton who left after making payments on his life insurance policy for the next two and a half years. There was a chicken sexer from Petaluma who left convinced we would all be back in three months. There was a well-dressed older woman from Burbank who left proudly, regally, with her head held up high in the air. "Viscount Oda's daughter," someone said. "Bellboy Goto's wife," said someone else. There was a man who had just been released from San Quentin who left already owing money to half the shopkeepers in town. "Time to move on," he said. There were college girls in black gabardine slacks—our older daughters—who left wearing American flag pins on their sweaters and Phi Beta Kappa keys dangling from gold chains around their necks. There were handsome young men in just-pressed chinos—our older sons—who left shouting the Berkeley fight song and talking about next year's big game. There was a newlywed couple in matching ski caps who left arm in arm and seemed to take no notice of anyone else. There was an elderly couple from Manteca who left having the same argument they'd been having since the day they first met. *If you say that one more time* ... There was an old man in a Salvation Army uniform from Alameda who left shouting out, "God is love! God is love!" There was a man from Yuba City who left with his half-Irish daughter, Eleanor, who had been delivered to him that morning by a woman he had deserted long ago. *He didn't even know of her existence until last week.* There was a tenant farmer from Woodland who left whistling Dixie after plowing under the last of his crops. There was a widow from Covina who left after giving power of attorney to a kind doctor who had offered to rent out her house. "I think I just made a big mistake." There was a young woman from San Jose who left carrying a bouquet of roses sent to her by an anonymous suitor from the neighborhood who had always admired her from afar. There were children from Salinas who left carrying bouquets of grass they had pulled up that morning from their front yards. There were children from San Benito and Napa who left wearing multiple layers of clothing in order to take as much as they could. There was a girl from a remote almond ranch in Oakdale who left shyly, fearfully, with her head pressed into her mother's skirt, for she had never seen so many people in her life. There were three young boys from the orphanage in San Francisco who left looking forward to taking their first ride on a train. There was an eight-year-old boy from Placerville who left carrying a small duffel bag packed for him by his foster mother, Mrs. Luhrman, who had told him he'd be back by the end of the week. "Now you go and have yourself a good time," she'd said. There was a boy from Lemon Cove who left clinging to his older sister's back. "It's the only way I could get him out of the house." There was a girl from Kernville who left carrying a small cardboard suitcase filled with candy and toys. There was a girl from Heber who left bouncing a red rubber ball. There were five sisters from Selma—the Matsumoto girls—who left fighting over their father, as always, and already one of them had a black eye. There were twin boys from Livingston who left wearing matching white slings on their right arms even though they were perfectly fine. "They've been wearing those things for *days*," their mother said. There were six brothers from a strawberry ranch in Dominguez who left wearing cowboy boots so they wouldn't get bitten by snakes. "Rough terrain ahead," one said. There were children who left thinking they were going camping. There were children who left thinking they were going hiking, or to the circus, or swimming for the day at the beach. There was a boy on roller skates who did not care where it was he was going as long as there were paved streets. There were children who left one month short of their high school graduation. *I was going to go to Stanford.* There was a girl who left knowing she would have been valedictorian at Calexico High. There were children who left still baffled by decimals and fractions. There were children from Mrs. Crozier's eighth-grade English class in Escondido who left relieved that they wouldn't have to take next week's big test. *I didn't do the reading.* There was a boy from Hollister who left carrying a white feather in his pocket and a book of North American birds given to him by his classmates on his last day at school. There was a boy from Byron who left carrying a tin pail filled with dirt. There was a girl from Upland who left carrying a limp rag doll with black button eyes. There was a girl from Caruthers who left dragging a jump rope behind her of which she refused to let go. There was a boy from Milpitas who left worrying about his pet rooster, Frank, whom he'd given to the family next door. "Do you think they'll eat him?" he asked. There was a boy from Ocean Park who left with the unearthly howls of his dog, Chibi, still echoing in his ears. There was a boy in a Cub Scout uniform from Mountain View who left carrying a mess kit and canteen. There was a girl from Elk Grove who left tugging on her father's sleeve and saying, "Papa, go home, go home." There was a girl from Hanford who left wondering about her Alaskan pen pal, June. *I hope she remembers to write.* There was a boy from Brawley who had just learned how to tell time who left constantly checking his watch. "It keeps on changing," he said. There was a boy from Parlier who left carrying a blue flannel blanket that still smelled of his room. There was a girl in long pigtails from a small town in Tulare who left carrying a thick stick of pink chalk. She stopped once to say good-bye to the people lined up on the sidewalk and then, with a quick flick of her wrist, she waved them away and began skipping. She left laughing. She left without looking back.

A DISAPPEARANCE

The Japanese have disappeared from our town. Their houses are boarded up and empty now. Their mailboxes have begun to overflow. Unclaimed newspapers litter their sagging front porches and gardens. Abandoned cars sit in their driveways. Thick knotty weeds are sprouting up through their lawns. In their backyards the tulips are wilting. Stray cats wander. Last loads of laundry still cling to the line. In one of their kitchens—Emi Saito's—a black telephone rings and rings.

DOWNTOWN, on Main Street, their dry cleaners are still shuttered. *For Lease* signs hang in their windows. Unpaid bills and business receipts drift by in the breeze. Murata Florist is now Flowers by Kay. The Yamato Hotel has become the Paradise. Fuji Restaurant will be reopening under new management by the end of the week. Mikado Pool Hall is closed. Imanashi Transfer is closed. Harada Grocery is closed, and in its front window hangs a handwritten sign none of us can remember having seen there before—*God be with you until we meet again,* it reads. And of course, we cannot help but wonder: Who put up the sign? Was it one of them? Or one of us? And if it was one of us, which one of us was it? We ask ourselves this as we press our foreheads to the glass and squint into the darkness, half expecting Mr. Harada himself to come barreling out from behind the counter in his faded green apron, urging upon us a stalk of asparagus, a perfect strawberry, a sprig of fresh mint, but there is nothing there to be seen. The shelves are empty. The floors, neatly swept. The Japanese are gone.

OUR MAYOR has assured us there is no need for alarm. "The Japanese are in a safe place," he is quoted as saying in this morning's *Star Tribune.* He is not at liberty, however, to reveal where that place is. "They wouldn't be safe now, would they, if I told you where they were." But what place could be safer, some of us ask, than right here, in our own town?

THEORIES, of course, abound. Perhaps the Japanese were sent out to the sugar beet country—Montana or the Dakotas, where the farmers will need help badly with their crops this summer and fall. Or perhaps they've assumed new Chinese identities in a faraway city where nobody knows who they are. Perhaps they're in jail. "My honest opinion?" says a retired Navy corpsman. "I think they're out there on the ocean, zigzagging past the torpedoes. They've all been shipped back to Japan for the duration of the war." A science teacher at the local high school says she lies awake every night fearing the worst: they've been herded into cattle cars and they're not coming back, or they're on a bus with no windows and that bus is not stopping, not tomorrow, not next week, not ever, or they're marching single file across a long wooden bridge and when they get to the other side of that bridge they'll be gone. "I'll be thinking these things," she says, "and then I'll remember—they already *are* gone."

YOU CAN STILL SEE the official notices nailed to the telephone poles on the street corners downtown, but already they are beginning to tatter and fade, and after last week's heavy spring rains only the large black letters on top— *Instructions to All Persons of Japanese Ancestry*—are still legible. But what it was, exactly, that these instructions spelled out, none of us can clearly recall. One man vaguely remembers a no-pets directive, as well as a designated point of departure. "I think it was the YMCA on West Fifth Street," he says. But he's not sure. A waitress at the Blue Ribbon Diner says she made several attempts to read the notice the morning it was posted but found it impossible to get up close. "All the telephone poles were surrounded by little clusters of concerned Japanese," she tells us. What struck her was how quiet everyone was. How calm. Some of the Japanese, she says, were slowly nodding their heads. Others took notes. None of them said a word. Many of us admit that although we passed by the notices every day on our way into town, it never occurred to us to stop and read one. "They weren't for us," we say. Or, "I was always in a rush." Or, "I couldn't make out a thing because the writing was just so small."

IT IS OUR CHILDREN who seem to have taken the disappearance of the Japanese most to heart. They talk back to us more than usual. They refuse to do their homework. They are anxious. They fuss. At night formerly brave sleepers are now afraid to turn off the light. "Every time I close my eyes I can see them," one child says. Another has questions. Where can he go to find them? Is there school where they are? And what should he do with Lester Nakano's sweater? "Keep it or throw it away?" Over at Lincoln Elementary an entire class of second graders has become convinced that their Japanese schoolmates have gotten lost in the forest. "They're eating acorns and leaves and one of them forgot her jacket and she's cold," one girl says. "She's shivering and crying. Or maybe she's dead." "She's dead," says the boy beside her. Their teacher says that the hardest part of her day now is taking roll. She points out the three empty desks: Oscar Tajima, Alice Okamoto, and her favorite, Delores Niwa. "So *shy*." Every morning she calls out their names, but of course, they never answer. "So I keep marking them absent. What else am I supposed to do?" "It's a shame," says the school crossing guard. "They were good kids. I'll miss them."

THERE ARE CERTAIN MEMBERS of our community, however, who were more than a little relieved to see the Japanese go. For we have read the stories in the papers, we have heard the whispered rumors, we know that secret caches of weapons were discovered in the cellars of Japanese farmers in towns not far from ours, and even though we would like to believe that most, if not all, of the Japanese here in our own town were good, trustworthy citizens, of their absolute loyalty we could not be sure. "There was just so much about them we didn't know," says one mother of five. "It made me uneasy. I always felt like there was something they were trying to hide." When asked if he had felt safe living across the street from the Miyamotos, a worker at the ice factory replies, "Not really." He and his wife were always very careful around the Japanese, he explains, because "we just weren't sure. There were good ones and bad ones, I guess. I got them all mixed up." But most of us find it difficult to believe that our former neighbors could have posed a threat to our town. A woman who used to rent to the Nakamuras says they were the best tenants she's ever had. "Friendly. Polite. And so clean, you could practically eat off their floors." "And they lived American, too," says her husband. "Not a Japanese touch anywhere. Not even a vase."

WE BEGIN TO RECEIVE reports of lights left on in some of the Japanese houses, and animals in distress. A listless canary glimpsed through the Fujimotos' front window. Dying koi in a pond over at the Yamaguchis'. And everywhere, the dogs. We offer them bowls of water, pieces of bread, leftover scraps from our tables, the butcher sends over a fresh cut of filet mignon. The Koyamas' dog sniffs politely and then turns away. The Uedas' dog bolts past us and before we can stop her she's out the front gate. The

Nakanishis' dog—a Scottish terrier that is a dead ringer for the President's little black dog, Fala—bares his teeth and won't let us anywhere near. But the rest come running out to greet us, as though they have always known us, and then follow us home, and within days we have found them new owners. One family says they would be more than happy to adopt a Japanese dog. Another asks if there are any collies. The wife of a young soldier who was just called up for duty takes home the Maruyamas' black-and-tan beagle, Duke, who follows her from room to room and won't let her out of his sight. "He's my protector now," she says. "We get along just fine." Sometimes, though, in the middle of the night, she can hear him whimpering in his sleep and she wonders if he is dreaming of them.

A FEW OF THE THEM, we soon learn, are still with us. Gambling boss Hideo Kodama, a prisoner at the county jail. An expectant mother at the public hospital who is more than ten days overdue. *That baby just doesn't want to drop.* A thirty-nine-year-old woman at the asylum for the insane who wanders the halls all day long in her night-gown and slippers, quietly mumbling to herself in Japanese, which nobody else can understand. The only words of English she knows are "water" and "Go home." Twenty years ago, the doctor tells us, her two young children were killed in a fire while she was out in the fields with another man. Her husband took his own life the next day. Her lover left her. "And ever since then she just hasn't been the same." On the southern edge of town, at the Clearview

Sanitorium, a twelve-year-old boy lies in a bed by a window, slowly dying of tuberculosis of the spine. His parents paid him one last visit the day before they left town and now he is all alone.

WITH EACH PASSING DAY the notices on the telephone poles grow increasingly faint. And then, one morning, there is not a single notice to be found, and for a moment the town feels oddly naked, and it is almost as if the Japanese were never here at all.

MORNING GLORIES BEGIN to grow wild in their gardens. Honeysuckle vines spread from one yard to the next. Beneath untended hedges, forgotten shovels rust. A lilac bush blossoms deep purple beneath the Oteros' front window and then disappears the next day. A lemon tree is dug up over at the Sawadas'. Locks are jimmied off of front and back doors. Cars are stripped. Attics raided. Stovepipes pried loose. Boxes and trunks are hauled up out of basements and loaded into pickup trucks under cover of night. Doorknobs and lighting fixtures go missing. And out on Third Avenue, in the pawn and second-hand shops, exotic items from the Far East briefly surface before making their way into some of our homes. A stone lantern appears among the azaleas in a prizewinning garden on Mapleridge Road. A painted paper scroll replaces a picture of a naked bather in a living room on Elm. On block after block, Oriental rugs materialize beneath our feet. And on the west side of town, among the more fashionable set of young mothers who daily frequent the park, chopstick hair ornaments have suddenly become all the rage. "I try not to think about where they came from," says one mother as she rocks her baby back and forth on a bench in the shade. "Sometimes it's better not to know."

FOR SEVERAL WEEKS some of us continue to hold out hope that the Japanese might return, because nobody said it would be forever. We look for them at the bus stop. At the florist. As we're walking past the radio repair shop on Second Avenue formerly known as Nagamatsu Fish. We glance out our windows repeatedly just in case our gardeners have snuck back, unannounced, into our yards. *There's always a slight chance Yoshi might be out there raking leaves.* We wonder if it wasn't somehow all our fault. Perhaps we should have petitioned the mayor. The governor. The President himself. *Please let them stay.* Or simply knocked on their doors and offered to help. If only, we say to ourselves, we'd *known.* But the last time any of us saw Mr. Mori at the fruit stand he was just as friendly as ever. "He never mentioned to me that he was going away," one woman says. Three days later, however, he was gone. A cashier at the Associated Market says that the day before the Japanese disappeared they were stocking up on food "like there was no tomorrow." One woman, she says, bought more than twenty tins of Vienna sausage. "I didn't think to ask her why." Now, of course, she wishes she had. "I just want to know they're all right."

HERE AND THERE, in scattered mailboxes all throughout town, our first letters begin to arrive from the Japanese. A boy on Sycamore receives a short note from Ed Ikeda, who was once the fastest sprinter at Woodrow Wilson Junior High. *Well, here we are at the reception center. I never saw so many Japanese in my life. Some people do nothing but sleep all afternoon long.* A girl on Mulberry Street hears from her former classmate Jan. *They are keeping us here for a little while longer and then they are sending us over the mountains. Hope to hear from you soon.* The mayor's wife receives a brief postcard from her loyal maid, Yuka, who showed up at her door on her second day off the boat. *Don't forget to air out the blankets at the end of the month.* The wife of the assistant pastor at the United Methodist Church opens a letter addressed to her husband, which begins, *Darling, am all right,* and her whole world goes suddenly dark. *Who is Hatsuko?* Three blocks away, in a yellow house on Walnut, a nine-year-old boy reads a letter from his best friend, Lester—*Did I leave my sweater in your room?*—and for the next three nights he is unable to sleep.

PEOPLE BEGIN to demand answers. Did the Japanese go to the reception centers voluntarily, or under duress? What is their ultimate destination? Why were we not informed of their departure in advance? Who, if anyone, will intervene on their behalf? Are they innocent? Are they guilty? Are they even really gone? Because isn't it odd that no one we know actually saw them leave?

You'd think, says a member of the Home Front Commandos, that one of us would have seen something, heard something. "A warning shot. A muffled sob. A line of people disappearing into the night." Perhaps, says a local air-raid warden, the Japanese are still with us, and are watching us from the shadows, scrutinizing our faces for signs of grief and remorse. Or maybe they've gone into hiding beneath the streets of our town and are plotting our eventual demise. Their letters, he points out, could easily have been faked. Their disappearance, he suggests, is a ruse. Our day of reckoning, he warns, is yet to come.

THE MAYOR URGES us all to be patient. "We'll let you know what we can when we can," he tells us. There was disloyalty on the part of some, time was short, and the need for action was great. The Japanese have left us willingly, we are told, and without rancor, per the President's request. Their spirits remain high. Their appetite is good. Their resettlement is proceeding according to plan. These are, the mayor reminds us, extraordinary times. We are part of the battlefront now, and whatever must be done to defend the country must be done. "There will be some things that people will see," he tells us. "And there will be some things that people won't see. These things happen. And life goes on."

THE FIRST BLAST of summer. Leaves droop on the branches of the magnolia trees. Sidewalks bake in the sun. Shouts fill the air as the final school bell rings and classes once more come to a close. Mothers' hearts fill with despair. *Not again,* they groan. Some of them begin looking for new nannies to take care of their young children. Others advertise for new cooks. Many hire new gardeners and maids: sturdy young women from the Philippines, thin bearded Hindus, short squat Mexicans from Oaxaca who, though not always sober, are friendly enough—*Buenos días,* they say, and *Sí, cómo no?*—and willing to mow their lawns for cheap. Most take the plunge and drop off their laundry with the Chinese. And even though their linens might not come back to them perfectly pressed, and their hedges are sometimes unruly, they do not let it bother them, for their attention has turned to other things: the search for a missing boy named Henry, last seen balancing on a log at the edge of the woods ("He's gone away to join the Japanese," our children tell us), the capture of seven soldiers from our town in the battle of Corregidor, a lecture at the annual Pilgrim Mothers' Club luncheon by recent Nazi refugee Dr. Raoul Aschendorff, entitled "Hitler: Today's Napoleon?" which draws a standing-room-only crowd.

AS THE WAR rages on families begin to leave their homes less and less. Gasoline is rationed. Tinfoil, saved. Victory gardens are planted on weed-strewn vacant lots and in kitchen after kitchen, the green bean casserole quickly loses its appeal. Mothers rip up their girdles to donate to the rubber drive and exhale fully for the first time in years. "Sacrifices must be made," they exclaim. Cruel fathers cut down their children's tire swings from the trees. The China Relief Committee reaches its target goal of ten thousand dollars and the mayor himself personally wires the good news to Madame Chiang Kai-shek. The assistant pastor spends another night out on the couch. Several of our children attempt to write to their Japanese friends but can't think of anything to say. Others don't have the heart to deliver the bad news. *There's a new boy sitting at your desk in Miss Holden's class. I can't find your sweater. Yesterday your dog got run over by a car.* A girl on North Fremont is discouraged by the postman, who tells her that only a traitor would dare exchange letters with the Japanese.

NEW PEOPLE BEGIN to move into their houses. Okies and Arkies who've come out west for the war work. Dispossessed farmers from the Ozarks. Dirt-poor Negroes with their bundles of belongings fresh up from the South. Vagrants and squatters. Country folk. Not our kind. *Some of them can't even spell.* They work ten and fifteen hours a day in the ammunitions plants. They live three and four families to a house. They wash their laundry out of doors, in tin tubs in their front yards. They let their women and children run wild. And on the weekends, when they sit out on their porches smoking and drinking until late in the night, we begin to long for our old neighbors, the quiet Japanese.

AT THE END of summer the first rumors of the trains begin to reach us from afar. They were ancient, people say.

Relics from a distant era. Dusty day coaches with coal-fired steam engines and antique gas lamps. Their rooftops were covered with bird droppings. Their windowpanes blackened by shades. They passed through town after town but made no stops. They blew no whistles. They traveled only after dusk. *Ghost trains,* say those who saw them. Some say they were climbing up through the narrow mountain passes of the Sierra Nevadas: Altamont, Siskiyou, Shasta, the Tehachapi. Some say they were heading toward the western edge of the Rockies. A timekeeper at the station in Truckee reports seeing a blind lifted and a woman's face briefly revealed. *"Japanese,"* he says. Although it happened so quickly it was impossible to know for sure. The train was unscheduled. The woman looked tired. She had short black hair and a small round face and we wonder if she was one of ours. Laundryman Ito's wife, perhaps. Or the old woman who sold flowers every weekend on the corner of Edwards and State. *We just called her the flower lady.* Or someone we might have passed by countless times on the street without really noticing at all.

IN AUTUMN there is no Buddhist harvest festival on Main Street. No Chrysanthemum Feast. No parade of bobbing paper lanterns at dusk. No children in long-sleeved cotton kimonos singing and dancing to the wild beating of the drums until late in the night. Because the Japanese are gone, that's all. "You worry about them, you pray for them, and then you just have to move on," says one elderly pensioner who lived next door to the Ogatas for more than ten years. Whenever he starts to feel lonely he goes outside and sits on a bench in the park. "I listen to the birds until I begin to feel better again," he says. "Then I go home." Sometimes several days go by and he doesn't think about the Japanese at all. But then he'll see a familiar face on the street—it's Mrs. Nishikawa from the bait shop, only why won't she wave back hello?—or a fresh rumor will float his way. *Rifles were found buried beneath the Koyanagis' plum tree. Black Dragon emblems were discovered in a Japanese house on Oak.* Or he'll hear footsteps behind him on the sidewalk but when he turns around there's nobody there. And then it will hit him all over again: the Japanese have left us and we don't know where they are.

BY THE FIRST FROST their faces begin to blend and blur in our minds. Their names start to elude us. *Was it Mr. Kato or Mr. Sato?* Their letters cease to arrive. Our children, who once missed them so fervently, no longer ask us where they are. Our youngest can barely remember them. "I think I saw one once," they say to us. Or, "Didn't they all have black hair?" And after a while we notice ourselves speaking of them more and more in the past tense. Some days we forget they were ever with us, although late at night they often surface, unexpectedly, in our dreams. *It was the nurseryman's son, Elliot. He told me not to worry, they're doing all right, they're getting plenty to eat and playing baseball all day long.* And in the morning, when we wake, try as we might to hang on to them, they do not linger long in our thoughts.

A YEAR ON and almost all traces of the Japanese have disappeared from our town. Gold stars glimmer in our front windows. Beautiful young war widows push their strollers through the park. On shady paths along the edge of the reservoir, dogs on long leashes strut. Downtown, on Main Street, the daffodils are blooming. New Liberty Chop Suey is crowded with workers from the shipping yard on their lunch break. Soldiers home on leave are prowling the streets and business at the Paradise Hotel is brisk. Flowers by Kay is now Foley's Spirit Shop. Harada Grocery has been taken over by a Chinese man named Wong but otherwise looks exactly the same, and whenever we walk past his window it is easy to imagine that everything is as it was before. But Mr. Harada is no longer with us, and the rest of the Japanese are gone. We speak of them rarely now, if at all, although word from the other side of the mountains continues to reach us from time to time—entire cities of Japanese have sprung up in the deserts of Nevada and Utah, Japanese in Idaho have been put to work picking beets in the fields, and in Wyoming a group of Japanese children was seen emerging, shivering and hungry, from a forest at dusk. But this is only hearsay, and none of it necessarily true. All we know is that the Japanese are out there somewhere, in one place or another, and we shall probably not meet them again in this world.

ACKNOWLEDGMENTS

This novel was inspired by the life stories of Japanese immigrants who came to America in the early 1900s. I have drawn upon a large number of historical sources, and although there is not room here to mention them all, I would like to list those that were most important to me in my research. I am particularly indebted to Kazuo Ito's *Issei: A History of Japanese Immigrants in North America* and Eileen Sunada Sarasohn's *The Issei* and *Issei Women.* Other important books include: *East Bay Japanese for Action Presents "Our Recollections"*; Stan Flewelling's *Shirakawa*; Audrie Girdner and Anne Loftis's *The Great Betrayal*; Evelyn Nakano Glenn's *Issei, Nisei, War Bride*; Yuji Ichioka's *The Issei*; *Impounded*, edited by Linda Gordon and Gary Y. Okihiro; Lauren Kessler's *Stubborn Twig*; Akemi Kikumura's *Through Harsh Winters*; Minoru Kiyota's *Beyond Loyalty*; *Lafcadio Hearn's Japan*, edited by Donald Richie; Ellen Levine's *A Fence Away from Freedom*; Tomoko Makabe's *Picture Brides*, Sayo Masuda's *Autobiography of a Geisha*; David Mas Masumoto's *Country Voices* and *Epitaph for a Peach*; Valerie J. Matsumoto's *Farming the Home Place*; Mei Nakano's *Japanese American Women*; *Only What We Could Carry*, edited by Lawson Fusao Inada; Donald Richie's *The Inland Sea*; Bernard Rudofsky's *The Kimono Mind*; Dr. Junichi Saga's *Memories of Silk and Straw* and *Memories of Wind and Waves*; Etsu Inagaki Sugimoto's *A Daughter of the Samurai*; Sonia Shinn Sunoo's *Korean Picture Brides*; Ronald Takaki's *Strangers from a Different Shore*; Nagatsuka Takashi's *The Soil;* Linda Tamura's *The Hood River Issei;* John Tateishi's *And Justice for All;* Dorothy Swaine Thomas's *The Salvage;* Yoshiko Uchida's *Desert Exile;* Wakako Yamauchi's *Songs My Mother Taught Me;* and Won Kil Yoon's *The Passage of a Picture Bride.* Several lines of the mayor's dialogue on page 124 were taken from a Department of Defense news briefing given by Secretary of Defense Donald Rumsfeld on October 12, 2001. I would also like to acknowledge my debt to Mary Swan, whose short story "1917" provided the inspiration for the first chapter of my novel.

I am deeply grateful to Nicole Aragi, without whose unwavering commitment this book could not have been written; to Jordan Pavlin for her elegant editorial advice; to Kathy Minton and Isaiah Sheffer at Symphony Space for their long and continued support; and to the John Simon Guggenheim Memorial Foundation for its generous assistance. Thank you also to Leslie Levine, Russell Perreault, Michelle Somers, and Christie Hauser. Special thanks to my family and to my best friend, Kabi Hartman. And to Andy Bienen, with love.

A NOTE ABOUT THE AUTHOR

Julie Otsuka was born and raised in California.
She is the author of the novel *When the Emperor Was
Divine* and is a recipient of the Asian American
Literary Award, the American Library Association
Alex Award, and a Guggenheim fellowship.
She lives in New York City.

A NOTE ON THE TYPE

This book was typeset in a digitized version of
Engravers' Oldstyle 205. A transitional typeface
based on French copperplate lettering and on the
Cochin letterform, it was originally designed in
the eighteenth century. Later adapted by Sol Hess,
it was revised by Matthew Carter for Bitstream.

COMPOSED BY *North Market Street Graphics,*
Lancaster, Pennsylvania
PRINTED AND BOUND BY *Berryville Graphics,*
Berryville, Virginia
DESIGNED BY *Iris Weinstein*